D1454235

WE DON'T KNOW WHAT WE'RE DOING

WE DON'T KNOW
WHAT WE'RE DOING

STORIES BY
THOMAS MORRIS

FABER & FABER

First published in 2015
by Faber & Faber Ltd
Bloomsbury House
74–77 Great Russell Street
London WC1B 3DA

Typeset in Sabon LT Std by Faber & Faber Ltd
Printed and bound by CPI Group (UK) Ltd, Croydon CR0 4YY

A CIP record for this book
is available from the British Library

ISBN 978–0–571–31701–1

These stories are works of fiction.
Any resemblance to real life is purely inevitable.

There has to be talking. That's what people do, they talk.

Any fool can cry wolf; to cry sheep is inspired.

The watermills belonged to the manor of Singraven near Denekamp . . . While the watermills do exist, the setting is Ruisdael's invention: there are no hills near Denekamp.

From a note at the National Gallery for Van Ruisdael's *Two Watermills and an Open Sluice at Singraven*

CONTENTS

BOLT

I'm filling my satchel with Butterkist popcorn and soon-to-be-gone-off Dairy Milk when she comes into the store. She looks at my bag, puts a hand over her eyes, and says in a costume-drama voice, 'I've seen nothing, Andy. Continue as you are.' She walks a steady pace through the New Releases aisle, the sound of her heels muffled by the red carpet. She used to come in with her husband, but I haven't seen him in months.

The shelves are almost bare, and all week the regulars have commiserated me, expressed their regrets at the situation. Sometimes I'll say in pretend anger, 'I'm mad as hell and I'm not gonna take it any more!' And sometimes I'll say not much at all, just nod and accept their apologies and money.

But I'm not desperate yet. Rent at Hannah's mother's is low, less than low – it's just bills, and some contribution to food that she often won't even accept. I think it's partly guilt at the way her daughter treated me, but I reckon she also enjoys the company. And we do get on – she's like Hannah without the neurotic stuff.

*

The woman makes a funny trotting noise with her mouth as she walks through the Ex-Rentals aisle, then looks at me and laughs. Aside from the closure, the horse has been the talk of the day. There was a wedding up by the castle, and the couple had booked a horse-drawn cart. Martin, the town's only homeless man, told me about it earlier.

'I seen it!' he said, like some sea captain describing a mermaid sighting. 'The guys unhooked the horse to fix a wheel on the cart and – bang! – she was gone, just like that. It ran through the town, on its own – cartless! Women were screaming, and children cheered wildly. But when it reached the red light by the shopping centre, it just stopped. It saw the red light and wouldn't move. And before the lights turned green, the owners caught up with it and reined the bugger back up!'

'But why did it stop at the lights?' I asked.

'I dunno,' he said. 'You'd have to ask the horse.'

The woman pulls to a sudden halt at the Classics section, with her elbows resting at her side, her arms out in front, her hands bent like hooves. She's the town's only psychiatrist and she's pretending to be a horse.

'Is this one any good, Andy?' she says, holding up a video. Hannah used to have sessions with her when she was younger, and told me she found her 'creepy'. But I've always liked the psychiatrist. She looks good for her age – late forties, I'd guess – and the store always smells nice after she leaves.

'What is it?' I say.

'*The Apartment.*'

'Ah. Romance at its most anti-romantic – that is the Billy Wilder stamp of genius, and this Academy Award winner from 1960 is no exception.'

She looks down at the video.

'That's just the blurb, Andy,' she says. 'Is it any good?'

'I haven't seen it,' I say. 'I just know all the synopses.'

'So now you confess.'

'Yeah. Like a man on death row.'

She puts the video down, then realises it's the wrong shelf. She goes to put it back, but I tell her not to bother.

'You can't beat VHS, can you?' she says. She sweeps a hand through her brown-grey hair, and bracelets jangle on her wrist.

'Oh you can,' I say. 'The amount of time I've wasted in front of a video player waiting for the bloody thing to rewind—'

My phone vibrates before I finish my speech. There's a message from Hannah's mum: dinner's in the micro-wave, I can heat it up when I get in.

Back at the till, I take some chocolate from my satchel. It's late in the evening and my sugar levels are low. Hannah's mother has taught me all about this – the need for regular eating, and the importance of listening to my body. She's good like that; she takes an interest.

'How you feeling about it all then?' the psychiatrist says, trotting over to me.

I lift my head above the counter, and put a hand to my mouth to hide the chomping.

'Sad to be leaving,' I say. 'But it's a good chance to do something else, you know. I might go travelling for a bit.'

'Where you thinking, Andy?'

It feels nice to hear her say my name. But I've seen enough mental-hospital films to know it's all part of the psychiatrist's toolkit.

'Well?'

I gesture at my mouth to show I need to finish chewing before I speak. It'd be nice to say her name too, but I don't know what it is. She did tell me once, but I can't remember. My boss doesn't know her name either, and she's been coming in for too long for us to ask her straight out.

I swallow the last melted lump of Dairy Milk and I can feel the chocolate coating my teeth.

'I quite fancy Australia,' I say. 'Did you ever see *Picnic at Hanging Rock*?' I think her name might be Andrea, but I can't be sure – she's always used her husband's membership card.

'Don't bother,' she says. 'I lived in Melbourne for three years. It's full of racists and the sun goes down at six. Winter or summer, it's dark when you finish work.'

'It looks amazing, though,' I say. 'All that space and freedom. And—'

'You should go to Berlin,' she says. 'It's a great city. And the people there actually value their freedom, you know? They fought for it.'

I think of *Good Bye Lenin!*, of old men with hammers at the wall, of hands touching through the gaps where bricks had been, of the boy's mother sleeping through it all.

'But I don't speak German,' I say.

'Yeah, well,' she says, 'neither do they.'

I nod, like a pupil receiving instruction.

'What are you doing tonight then?' she says. She raises her left foot and caresses the back of her right calf with it. If I were a woman, would I wear heels to a video store?

'Tonight?' I say. 'Nothing.' I run my tongue across my teeth and they feel grainy with the chocolate.

'Your last night and you're doing nothing?'

'Correct.'

'*Verrry* interesting,' she says, all Transylvanian.

Since Hannah left I've barely been out. All the people I know around here are *her* friends, and now we're not together they don't particularly want to see me. Besides, most of the good ones have left the town too. So if I'm not working, I just stay in the house and watch *Wallander* with Hannah's mum.

The woman continues her way round the store, picking up videos and putting them down.

'Everything's a pound,' I call out to her.

'I saw the signs,' she says.

The strip-light flickers. It clicks and clanks like there's

a bee trapped in there. I'd change the bulb but there's really no point.

Hannah once told me that at each of her sessions the psychiatrist tried to make her cry. She told her that Hannah's family didn't speak about their issues, about the divorce, and that's why Hannah had the problems she had. According to Hannah, the crying didn't help, though. She'd just leave more upset than when she arrived.

I walk through the shop, straightening the videos.

'Where's the boss then, Andy?' the psychiatrist says when I get to her aisle. 'Isn't she here for the big goodbye?'

'It was her mate's wedding earlier,' I say. 'She's at the party now. We have to come back in on Sunday anyway – to pack everything up – so we'll get to say goodbye then.'

'I meant a big goodbye to valued customers like me, Andy. Am *I* not valued?'

'Very much so,' I say. Tom Hanks on the cover of *Big* stares out at me, as if he knows I've been stealing chocolate. 'But I'm the only one here, I'm afraid.'

She smiles. 'I suppose you'll have to do, Andy. Anyway, don't mind me. You must be closing up in a bit?'

'No worries,' I say. 'Take your time.'

She picks up *The Apartment* again. 'What do you think then? Fancy watching it?'

'In here?' I say.

'No, no. At my place.'

I think of the meat and vegetables going cold in the microwave, the gravy congealing.

'Ah, come on,' she says. 'Come keep an old woman company.'

Outside, autumn lurks like a mugger. You can feel the change in the air, on your cheeks. My boss told me that before it was a video shop the place used to be a garage. The car park is where the forecourt used to be. And there's something about this bottom part of town that feels like a garage, like somewhere that people are only passing through.

When I pull down the shutters and padlock the bolt for the last time, I get the same feeling I used to have the night before a new school year. The feeling that'd make me lay my uniform out on my bedroom floor, down to the socks and shoes, and then lie in bed not sleeping.

Sitting against the wall, lit by Domino's Pizza, Martin holds a sign saying 'Need money for a penis reduction. Live free or die trying!' I unzip my bag and hand him four bags of Minstrels and a 'party-share size' bottle of Coke.

'I turn up for five years and this is all I get?' he says, and he readjusts his Man Utd bobble hat.

'It's more than I'm getting,' I say.

'What you gonna do now then?' he says.

'I'm going home,' I say.

The psychiatrist walks towards her car. With his teeth, Martin tears open a packet of Minstrels. He looks beyond me, to the car park.

'I meant now as in tomorrow,' he says. 'Like next week, what you gonna do?'

'I dunno,' I say.

He lifts the pack to his mouth and tips the Minstrels in.

'You should get another job, mun.'

'Good advice,' I say, and watch him chew.

He looks past me again, to the psychiatrist standing by the car. I turn around and look at her. Her hand is resting on top of the door.

'You best be off,' he whispers. 'Rule number seven: never be late for the shrink.'

She drives us up through town, past the castle, past the old furniture shop and past the closed-down post office. The car smells minty from the little green tree that hangs on the rear-view mirror. In the headlights, I can see horse shit on the road, flattened with tyre tracks. When we get up near the train station, a group of girls with heels the size of Coke cans run across the road, ignoring the lights. The psychiatrist pulls up sharply and beeps. And one of the girls slaps the bonnet.

'Motherfucker!' she shouts at us, and then she slowly crosses the road, staring at us the whole time.

'Nice,' says the psychiatrist. 'A healthy attitude to anger.'

'I bet the horse would have stopped,' I say.

'You reckon?' she says.

'Aye,' I say. 'He sounds like he had a *healthy* respect for authority.'

'Bollocks,' she says. 'There's no such thing.'

We drive past St Martin's Church, across St Martin's Road, and then up Caerphilly mountain.

'You hungry?' she says.

'Yeah.'

'I never cook,' she says. 'What do you think about getting a burger?'

The Snack Bar is a wooden shack at the top of the mountain. On the menu it says, 'Established in 1957 – We Are Older Than Motown And Coronation Street'. The psychiatrist orders us both a Mountain Monster Burger, and the guy tells us it will take five minutes. I bring out my wallet, but the psychiatrist insists on paying. The burger man laughs.

'Just let your mam treat you,' he says. He has a big face, and his pores are visible even though it's dark. We don't correct him, and he keeps on smiling.

'Where've you come from tonight then?' he asks. I say Caerphilly, and he starts going on about the horse.

'They came up here for their wedding photos, they did,' he says, pressing the burgers down with metal tongs. 'They came here on their first date so they wanted photos of themselves with a burger.'

'That sounds quite romantic,' the psychiatrist says, and I see her voice in front of us – a warm breath in cold air. The oil in the pan spits and spats.

'Aye,' says the burger man. 'Well, they came up here and they told me about the horse running off like that.

It's mad, innit? I can't believe it stopped at the lights.'

We agree that it's mad, and the burger man tells us how he's actually an actor and a writer, that this job is just something he does to pay the rent. He gives us a flyer for a play he's written and starring in. There's a picture of him wearing a silver suit, a ball of flames behind him, and the words 'Trial and Error' arched around his head in Comic Sans.

'What's it about?' the psychiatrist asks, squinting at the flyer in the burger shack's light.

'It's about a guy who's not very good at having relationships,' he says, and he takes a handful of onion slices from a tupperware box and tosses them into the pan. 'But it's very humoristic, though. It's a comedy, you know? Do you reckon you can come see it?'

I tell him I'll definitely try, and we take a seat at one of the tables. Down below us the streetlights chart the housing estates, and Caerphilly twinkles in the night.

'I like your coat,' the psychiatrist says.

'Thanks,' I say. 'My ex's mum bought it for me.'

The psychiatrist smiles, then looks past me, over to the town. She's got a concentrating look going on, as if she's remembering something. Hannah used to be the same. We'd be having a conversation and then she'd tune out and stare off at the corner of the ceiling.

'Caerphilly looks alright, doesn't it?' I say, looking behind me.

'Yeah. It's a paradox, though.'

'What is?'

'The fact that it only looks nice when you're away from it.'

I nod and try to pick out the castle down there among the lights. There's a sound of shoes over pebbles then – the man bringing us our burgers.

'Cracking, innit?' he says, casting a hand over the town.

'It is,' I say.

'I reckon I've got the best view in all of South Wales,' he says, and he sets a plastic ketchup bottle down on our table. 'Anyway, have a good 'un.'

I eat my burger greedily, glad to have something warming my hands. She nibbles hers slowly, like she's not even that hungry. And she keeps watching me, too. So after a few too many big bites, I go, 'Well, thank you, I really needed this.'

'You're welcome,' she says slowly, and she puts her food down, then taps a finger twice on her cheek. 'You've some sauce on your face.'

'Yeah?' I say. 'Well, it's the new style now. All the kids are doing it.'

*

Her hallway smells recently hoovered. She flips a switch and the place still feels dark. She lights incense in the living room and brings out red wine and purple tumblers from the kitchen.

'Do you want some?' she says.

'Why not,' I say, settling down on the orange couch.

'I'll turn the heating on now,' she says. 'The place will be like Spain in no time.'

We toast to new beginnings, though I don't know what new thing I'm actually beginning, and we both take sips.

On the wall above the telly there's a photo of a naked man and woman grappling each other.

'Can I use your toilet?' I say.

'Depends what you want it for.'

'Mostly toilet things.'

'Then yes,' she says. 'It's the second door on the left there.'

Like her, the bathroom smells delightful. There's pictures of flowers on the wall, and there's potpourri or something on the cistern. I go to wee but nothing comes out. This often happens. I'll go to the bathroom to escape awkwardness or take time out, but when I get there I'll forget this and try to piss.

I sit down on the toilet and send Hannah a sad face:

She hasn't replied to my last few texts.

The film is funnier than I thought it'd be. But it's really sad too. When Shirley MacLaine overdoses on sleeping tablets I can't watch. It seems too real.

'Here's a question,' I say, during a lull.

'Thanks for the warning,' she says, picking at her sleeve.

'Do you know what the two most popular phrases in US films are?'

'Let me think,' she says, and she tilts her head as if that'll help. 'Ummmmmmm. No.'

'Well,' I say. 'I'll educate you. The first is *Let's get out of here* and the second is *Try and get some sleep now*.'

'Interesting,' she says.

When Shirley MacLaine says to Jack Lemmon, 'Shut up and deal', we're both in tears. The psychiatrist wipes her eyes with her sleeve and goes to the kitchen. She comes back in with another bottle of wine, pours us large measures, then starts talking about her first husband. She says the marriage was *emotionally demanding*. I don't know what to say, so I edge the conversation back to her job. She tells me how draining she finds it. I ask her to diagnose me, and she laughs.

'I'm not very good at guessing personality types, Andy. That's not how counselling works. You seem a very nice boy, though. And that's a professional judgment, by the way.'

'I'm twenty-three,' I say.

'Yes, like I said: a boy.'

I look down at her carpet. It's green.

'Whatever happened to that girl you were with?' she says. 'I haven't seen her in ages.' She dips her hand deep into the popcorn to retrieve whatever's left. She puts some to her lips.

'Moved to London,' I say.

'Ah, an ambitious one then. Ambitious people always end up in the cities. Well, until they have a breakdown and come back. Are you two still together?'

'Not exactly.'

'Oh?'

'We're on a break.'

In reality, Hannah broke up with me three months ago and I spend my nights sending her aggressive, depressing emails, and keeping the same bedtime as the moon.

I've popcorn kernels stuck between my teeth and I dig in a sneaky fingernail to wedge them out.

'Do you resent her?' she asks.

I still have my finger in my mouth. I move it from the caverns of the molars to the wisdom tooth that's coming through at the back.

'Why would I?' I say, drying my finger on my work trousers.

'You moved all the way down from Bangor and then she went and left for London. And now you're still here, working in VideoZone.'

'Well, *not* working in VideoZone,' I say.

'Oh yeah, sorry,' she says. 'You know what I mean, though.'

She folds the empty bag of popcorn in half, and then in half again, and so on and on until it's a little red triangle. She picks it up and moves it in the air, like it's a boat sailing through a choppy sea.

'Yeah,' I say. 'But there's no work around here for her. She had to move.'

I reach over the arm of the couch, to my satchel, and take out another bag of popcorn.

Hannah and I started going out in the final year of university. When we finished our finals we both moved home. But after my father got jealous of all the time me and my stepmum spent together – that's when I had to leave. I didn't tell Hannah about any of this, though. I just came to Caerphilly to visit and never left. That was a year ago now, and I haven't heard from my father since.

'So you don't feel let down?' the psychiatrist says.

'Maybe a little.' I think of Dad coming at me with the hammer.

'That's the hallmark of maturity,' the psychiatrist says.

'What is?'

'Ambivalence.'

'I'm not ambivalent,' I say. 'I miss her.'

'No, no, I mean . . . to be able to see the good and the bad, to be double-minded.'

'Ah. Well, yes,' I say. 'I am frightfully mature for my age.'

For some reason she finds this very funny. I don't know why, but it makes her laugh. I generally know when I've said a good line – indeed, I have many – but that one really didn't deserve this reaction. She settles back on the couch, lies down, and rests her feet on my lap.

'You don't mind, do you?' she says.

'It's your house,' I say. 'You can put your feet wherever you want. I mean, this couch is probably, like, your office. Actually, do psychiatrists have offices?'

'They generally do,' she says. In her tights, her feet look webbed. 'But I'm a counsellor – and that's a different thing.'

'You're not a psychiatrist?'

'Nope. I started the training, but God, it was just too much work. Everyone round here thinks I'm a psychiatrist, though. I used to tell them I'm not, but I've just given up now.'

'I see,' I say. 'Do you ever do sessions from here, though?'

'I've learned not to bring work home with me,' she says. 'You know, after my first husband, I started seeing this counsellor from Cardiff and we'd do it in her living room. But she'd always fall asleep halfway through.'

I don't know if she's speaking about counselling or sex with a counsellor.

I say, '*And how did that make you feel?*'

She gives me a look. She's registered my comment but doesn't find it funny.

'It was strange, alright. I'd ask her was it me, but she'd say *no, go on*. I stopped going the third time it happened.'

'Weird,' I say.

'Yeah, but I felt guilty about not getting in touch.

It's never nice when someone stops seeing you without letting you know. But that's what I did. I couldn't face calling her about it.'

'Why did she fall asleep all the time?'

'Well, here's the thing,' she says. 'I was feeling really bad about it all. And even though she was the one being unprofessional, I couldn't help feel as if *I* was being unprofessional by not getting in touch. I started having dreams about seeing her in post offices and airport departure lounges and all these other obvious symbolic places. And then one day I was walking around Cardiff – and I was actually thinking about her, wondering how she was getting on – and then I saw her across the road on Queen Street. So I went over and I told her I was sorry I'd stopped going, but I just felt uncomfortable about her falling asleep.'

'What did she say?' I ask. I think of my mother asleep. The weight of her arm draped over the side of the couch; the way the light came in through the window.

'Well, we went and got some coffee, and she apologised about it all. She told me she'd been going through a bad time. Her husband had been violent. She said she really shouldn't have been doing the counselling herself, but she needed the money to get out. She said she'd worked through a lot of it with her own counsellor and now she was feeling much better about it all. She was glad to meet me, though, because she felt guilty about the way things had gone.'

I picture the chain of therapy: counsellor → counsellor → counsellor.

'Let me top you up there,' she says and refills my glass.

I don't tell her about my mother. Instead, I tell her about the night I found a man in a suit, lying on the side of the road, and how I thought he was dead. I called an ambulance and waited beside him in the dark for twenty minutes. But when the paramedics did their stuff, he woke up and told them to leave him alone. He said he'd just been having a nap.

Her bedroom is smaller than I expected. The place is spotless, like a show home, and her body is in really good shape for a woman her age. Hannah is so insecure about her body that all the sex happened in the dark. But the psychiatrist is confident – she removed her top and bra while we were in the doorway. And as expected, she smells wonderful.

As she moves down on me, I reach for my mobile on the bedside table. I call Hannah and set it to speakerphone. She won't answer, but when she listens to her voicemail she'll at least know how I'm spending my time.

I'm getting into it when I realise I've been very selfish so far. So I push the psychiatrist off and start doing all the things a guy should do. I don't think I'm very good at sex stuff, but she seems to enjoy it. Licking her, I think of licking batteries, and the jolt of the current running through my tongue. But before I know what's

happening, we've changed positions, and she's strad-
dling my waist and asking me to spank her.

Not really knowing what I'm doing, I awkwardly slap
her on the bum. She groans, and I can tell the groan
is exaggerated, deliberately encouraging. And there's
something about her encouragement that I find off-
putting. I spank her a few more times, and then she gets
down on her knees.

'Hit me in the face,' she says.

I feel myself seize up.

'You can do it as hard as you like,' she says, her head
leaning towards me.

'I don't want to hit you in the face,' I say. 'Why would
I want to hit you in the face?'

'Just a slap then,' she says. 'Go on. It'll only take a
second.'

She closes her eyes and swallows something that isn't
there. The tendons in her neck are thick, but the skin
looks thin, as if it's stretched too tightly around her
bones. I study her face. Her mascara has smudged, and
a thick black track bleeds across her temple. I raise my
hand. Her eyes are still closed, but she bites her lip now.
I've never hit anyone before, not properly. And with my
hand in the air, I don't know what I'm going to do. I
keep it there, aloft, for a moment, two moments, and
then, in the end, I just finger-flick her on the nose.

'Come on,' I say. 'Let's just do it.'

So we settle on sex the usual way – no funny business

– and when we're done, she cosies up to me and rests her head on my shoulder.

'How you doing?' I say.

She makes a noise, a sighing noise. 'You've no idea.'

I'm thinking of Hannah, of our first time in my college room, and how it feels like a very long time ago; how it seems like a line has just been drawn between then and now.

'No idea what?' I say.

'I dunno,' she says. 'I'm just too old for all this.'

'You're not old,' I say, running my hand over her leg.

I can feel the jut of her chin on my chest as she looks up at me.

'Am I meant to believe you *actually* think that?'

'Yeah,' I say.

The first time I took off Hannah's clothes, I was so turned on I came in my pants. She never found out, though; I hid it well.

'You're very kind,' she says. 'Seriously, though, I'm fifty-six. I could be your mother.'

I laugh, and then I think of Mum. A blemish of something, something hot, creeps up my neck.

'And how are you doing?' she says.

'Yeah, fine,' I say.

'Good good,' she says, and she reaches over and turns off the lamp.

I'm still thinking of Mum, and *The Apartment*, and Shirley MacLaine passed out on the bed.

'I was only six at the time,' I say.

'Shh,' she says, putting a finger to my lips. She whispers gently, stroking my neck. 'Shh, try and get some sleep now.'

When I wake up I've three missed calls from Hannah's mum, and two texts from Hannah. The first one says '*When are you moving out of my house?*' and the second has no words, only question marks:

????

The psychiatrist is fully dressed, standing in the doorway, and I'm under the covers, still naked. I can feel an erection stirring. Through the curtains there's a peek of morning light.

'How you feeling?' she says.

'Naked.'

'And your head?'

'Murky,' I say, scratching my arm. 'How about you?'

'I'm not too bad,' she says. 'I suppose there have to be *some* benefits to being a high-functioning alcoholic. Anyway, any plans for the day?'

I think about it.

'Nay,' I say.

'*Neighhhh!*' – she's back on the horse game again. 'Fancy a picnic later?'

'That'd be nice,' I say. 'Yeah, why not?'

She gives me a shirt of her ex-husband's to wear, and makes me scrambled egg on toast. We're in the kitchen, and every now and then she gives me a hug or a kiss on the back of the head. While I'm drinking a cup of tea, she massages my shoulders and tells me I have a lot of tension in my body.

'You've been very stressed,' she says. 'The shop closing down must be very hard for you.'

'I don't know,' I say, forking some egg into my mouth. 'Maybe.'

'Well, that part of your life is over now,' she says. 'It's time to start again.'

*

It's bright and cold out – as if the sun is just an inch too far away – and we're sitting at a picnic table across from the castle. The psychiatrist takes crisps from a giant bag we bought at Tesco, and eats two or three at a time.

'Here comes trouble,' she says when two ducks waddle up. She throws them a slice of Hovis each, and the bread lands on some freshly fallen leaves.

'Tell me a secret, little duckies,' she says. The ducks just nibble at the bread, chomping till it's all gone.

'Looks like they don't want to talk,' I say.

A little boy, in a coat like Paddington Bear's, walks past with his mother. He points at the ducks and goes '*quack!*'

'Now that's how you talk to ducks,' the psychiatrist says. She pierces the top of her Capri-Sun with the straw. 'Quality duck-talk.'

I take a slice of bread then cut some brie. I run my finger along the edge of the plastic knife and lick off the bits of cheese. The label on my shirt is starting to itch, so I smooth it down a little.

'It'll be cold tonight,' I say.

'How so?'

'Clear skies,' I say, gesturing with my brie sandwich. I take a bite and keep talking. 'Clear skies means no cloud coverage. And that means nothing to keep in the heat.'

'Sounds like the thought processes of a depressive,' she says.

'It's science,' I say.

'Well, Mother Nature must have had post-natal depression,' she says, and I snort with a laugh.

'Do you think you'll ever move back home then?' she says. There's an army of ducks around us now, all looking to be fed.

'Back to Bangor?' I say. I blow my nose into my hand, then rub it on the bench. 'I doubt it.'

'Well, what do you want to do?' she says. 'You've been out of uni a year now.'

'I know,' I say, watching the little boy throw bread to the ducks in the moat. I picture it going soggy, sinking in the water. 'I just don't know. I can't even remember what I wanted to do.'

I take out my phone and there's another message from Hannah's mother: '*R U OK?*'

'Let's get these buggers,' the psychiatrist says, and she hands me a wad of bread from the bag. 'Okay, step one: remove the dough from the middle and roll it up like a ball, like this.' She scrunches up the bread in her hand until it looks like a fist or a knotty heart.

I copy her and place the frame-crust down on the picnic table.

'No, no, pick that back up,' she says. 'That's the important part.' And then she takes her frame of bread and looks at the duck.

'Let's see if we can get this square bit around one of the ducks' necks,' she says. 'Like those games you get in fairgrounds, you know? And when it starts nibbling at the bread, that's when we'll throw the dough-ball.'

We do it for five minutes but it doesn't work. Throwing bread around a duck's neck is harder than it sounds.

'It's getting cold,' she says. 'Do you want to head back?

'Aye,' I say, though the temperature feels the same to me.

We go back to hers, she brings out her duvet, and we settle on the couch to watch more films. We watch *Sunset Boulevard* and then *Vanilla Sky*. Through the kitchen window, I can see the day is already over, the night is inky black. Ten minutes into *Good Bye Lenin!* we start having sex, and she keeps asking me to fuck her harder. I tell her to calm down, that I'm going as hard as I can. When we're done, we both sit up and she tells me that her first husband killed himself, and that the second husband had an affair. He left her two months ago, she says. I tell her I'm sorry – I don't know what else to say. She asks me to tell her what happened to my mother, but I don't want to talk about it.

'You need to,' she says.

'I don't,' I say.

'It's okay if you want to cry,' she says.

'I don't,' I say.

The film has stopped and we watch the screen go blue. The tape reaches the end of the reel, and it begins to rewind, begins to wind back to the start.

'Just popping to the toilet,' I say, getting up.

I go to her bedroom and get changed into my own clothes, into the VideoZone uniform. But I don't know what to do with her husband's shirt. I think about hanging it back in the wardrobe, but my neck has already dirtied the inside collar. And I don't want to leave the shirt on the bed, so I take it to the bathroom and bury it at the bottom of the laundry basket. It might be a while until she sees it.

When I come back in, she's on the couch, flicking through the TV channels. She's wearing her cardigan, buttons undone, a glimpse of breast still visible.

'Shall we get in pizza?' she says.

'I should probably get going,' I say.

She picks up the remote control, then puts it back down on the arm of the couch.

'Okay,' she says.

She offers me a lift but I tell her I'm fine to walk. She sees me to the door and kisses me on the forehead, tells me to be safe. It's misty out, and the ground is starting to stiffen with frost. I go along Mountain Road, the lights of the town disappearing as I move further down the mountain. Then I walk across St Martin's Road, past the church, all the while being careful not to slip. And though it's dark, the town's awake with people now. There's a queue of guys outside the Kings, as bouncers laugh and let in groups of girls who must be barely sixteen. *Come on,* the guys say, *it's fucking freezing.* A couple argue outside Chicken Land. The man wants to get a taxi into Cardiff, and the woman wants food. She's sat on the floor, her back against the window, refusing to move until she gets a burger. The man tells the taxi driver to wait, tells him this'll only take a minute. I walk through them, through the mist that's so low, and I keep going until I'm past Tesco and Martin, a blanket over him, eating a sandwich. I walk past the castle and the shopping centre and take a right at the lights, towards Hannah's house, back to Hannah's mum.

He is twenty-seven. The school he's teaching at is the same one he went to as a child, and his old teacher is headmaster now. He stays behind three evenings a week to prepare lessons, mark books, and make wall displays. When the place is empty, he uses the kids' toilets, the same bathrooms he used seventeen years ago. It feels almost wrong to bring his adult penis into the cubicles now, and it feels strange to wash his hands at the low sinks.

His wife is a swimming instructor at the sports centre. She once ran three marathons in a week for charity. Her feet blistered and she asked him to burst the blisters with a needle. He sterilised it with boiling water from the kettle, then sat at one end of the leather couch, while she lay with her foot resting on his lap. He held the foot, turned it gently. Just jab it in, she said. So he did, and the clear fluid streamed out. It's best to just do it, she said. It's no good having time to panic.

When they kiss he often thinks of their first time at Caerphilly rugby club. When he saw her, his friend Gareth said, 'If I could draw your perfect girl, she'd look just like that.' They were standing by the bar, the disco ball's light lapping twirls of silver. She was on the dance floor, wearing a black dress. She had long red hair, and she was laughing more than she was dancing.

'I can't talk to her,' he said.

Gareth grabbed his arm, and told him to man the fuck up. He pushed him onto the dance floor.

They were seventeen, and he'd only kissed three other girls before her. She tasted like Malibu and Coke.

It's been four months since he started at the school, and he hasn't been sleeping well. He dreams of losing teeth and being chased, and in the mornings he's disappointed by the obviousness of these dreams. In the night, his wife talks in her sleep. There are times when he wakes to hear her speaking a kind of Russian-sounding language. For a while he tried to stay awake when it happened. He thought she might disclose something important. Another man's name, perhaps. But no, just more gibberish. Where do they come from, he thinks, all these chains of nonsense?

One evening, at home after school, he showers and finds a grey pubic hair. It is long and when he pulls it out he's surprised by its strength. He always thought that grey hairs would feel different, weaker compared to others. He doesn't tell his wife. He googles '**grey hair cause**' and finds forums where concerned parties share their theories: stress, pollution, shampoo, genes, trauma, tooth-whitening products, lack of folic acid, ageing. He inspects his head in the hall mirror and finds another grey hair. He yanks it out. As a boy he spent entire afternoons staring out his bedroom window, watching his next-door neighbours as they lounged, barbecued, or cut the grass. The neighbours' garden was immaculate – the lawn bowling-green perfect. And then one summer they bought a Jack Russell. They only had it a fortnight before they gave it up to the pound. He remembers looking out from his window and watching as the woman cleaned up its shit, kneeling down and scrubbing the grass with silver wire wool and a bottle of Dettol.

'It's sad,' his mother said, looking out the window with him. 'I think she's having a nervous breakdown.'

*

His wife suggests they go out for dinner, but he tells her he has too much work. She offers to help, and orders in pizza. They sit on the living-room floor, on the thick cream carpet, and cut out pictures from the Next catalogue together. He's teaching the children to write stories, to invent and describe characters that feel real. Together, they eat pizza, cut out pictures of smiling men and women, and lay them on an A3 sheet of paper. His wife massages his shoulders and he kisses her on the neck. It's her day off, but her skin still smells of chlorine. He turns around, pushes her hair back and kisses her neck again.

She is thin and pale and beautiful. She looks at the pizza crusts in the box on the floor. We better laminate these pictures, she says. You wouldn't want to lose them.

His wife's parents had given them the deposit, and she said it would be stupid to pass up the chance – that they were only throwing money away by renting. His mother wasn't sure. She said Castle View was just an estate of Lego houses, that the walls were made of plaster, that she'd heard stories of people leaning on them and falling through.

'You can't even see the castle!' she said to him as they sat at her kitchen table. The floor tiles were cracked, lined black with dirt and dog hairs. 'Trust me, of all people,' she said, 'there's no rush to get a mortgage.'

He had wanted to say something, but he couldn't form the right thoughts or sentences, couldn't think of what to say.

He still can't believe how pristine these Castle View houses seem. The kitchen always smells of soap powder, and the bathroom air-freshened with Glade, but the cleanness feels like it comes from the house itself. The back garden is small – it only takes him ten minutes to trim the lawn with a strimmer. And when there's no washing on the line, the garden seems empty: just a palm tree in the corner, and the three sides of the enclosing wooden fence. Beyond the garden are the roofs of other houses. And beyond them, Caerphilly mountain skulks, washed-out green and brown and bare. When his mother first visited the house, she took a smoke in the garden, and looked out at the mountain.

'It looks like a big Christmas pudding, doesn't it?' she said. When he looks at it now, he thinks of words like *hump* and *bald* and *tired*.

On the evenings his wife doesn't work, they watch box sets and telly together. Between shows he asks about the people at the pool – different questions each time. Tonight he asks if they're good-looking. She shakes her head, undoes her ponytail, and resets her hair.

'Nah,' she says. 'This lot are a bunch of fat bastards.'

Her eyes are on an advert for Clover – a family picnicking in an empty green field. A new-looking rug and crackers and bread and yellow curls of butter. He once read that beautiful women fantasise about plain-looking and unattractive men. It makes the women feel good about themselves. To do a favour for someone, to slum it, turns them on. And he does think he is less attractive than when they first met. He is thickening around the waist, and he can feel his chest shake when he runs down the stairs. He isn't fat, exactly, but still – to someone like her, it must seem repellent.

On the evenings she doesn't work, they go to Morrisons, they go to the cinema and they go to her parents' house. He gets on well with her mother. She treats him like an adult, or at least some version of one. She doesn't challenge or question him like his own mother does. Her father he finds more difficult. But he's always found fathers odd: he doesn't know what the point of them is, he doesn't know what they're meant to do. But occasionally, some Saturdays, they watch Caerphilly play rugby. From the outside it could resemble, he thinks, a normal father–son relationship.

Sometimes, on weekends, he and his wife go to the pub with friends. And sometimes they go weeks without seeing them.

At night, he slips his hand down her pyjama trousers and strokes her. She takes longer and longer to get wet and he begins to think it's his fault. He pulls the bottoms down, tries to lick her, but with a hand on his shoulder she tells him to stop. 'I'm sorry,' he says. She reassures him, tells him not to worry.

He reads through her phone when she's in the shower or out at the shops. He never finds anything.

In class he hands out the laminated catalogue models, and asks the children what makes a character believable? There's silence, then one boy says: 'If they tell the truth.'

*

He still finds it hard to think of her as his wife. It's been a year since they married, and he imagined the whole thing would feel different, more tangible by now. He goes to google 'why does my girlfriend not get aroused?' but halfway through typing, Google auto-suggests 'why does my girlfriend hate me?' He looks it up. Someone says:

> my girlfriend acts like she doesnt care anymore and treats me like something she just stood in she dosent pay any bills and she keeps leaving me to go out with her friend she gets in moods and dosent talk to me for days and thats what shes doing now i cant live this anymore

There are fifteen replies. Some of them say she's probably bored, he should try to excite her, take her out somewhere nice. But most tell the guy to leave his girlfriend. The crux of the comments is: life's too short. Catch it before it goes.

He thinks: she doesn't hate me. She's just annoyed by the way I sometimes act. I can be too needy. And when she rejects me, I become cold and distant, then she finds it hard to know how to respond. I need to become constant. I need to be less pushy. I need to be patient.

One Thursday night, when she's at the pool, Gareth drops by. He brings a box of Magnums. They play FIFA on the Xbox and eat a Magnum each.

'How's life in graphic design?' he says.

'Graphic-designy,' Gareth says, his eyes not leaving the TV. 'And you? How's school?

'Fine,' he says. 'Schooly.'

They play FIFA for an hour, then he shows Gareth the office upstairs. It's empty except for a computer desk, a laminator, and a swivel chair. The walls are painted cream.

'Minimalist,' Gareth says, taking a bite from his second Magnum. 'I like it.'

'Cheers,' he says.

On the landing Gareth takes another bite, and a small piece of chocolate breaks off. It falls onto the carpet. Gareth gives him a squirming look.

He tuts and shakes his head. He talks to Gareth as if he's a kid from school. 'I'm not angry with you,' he says, softly. 'I'm just *very* disappointed.'

And then he laughs. He walks to the bathroom, takes some tissue, and returns to the landing. He carefully removes the chocolate as if it were a spider he doesn't want to kill.

'Can you see anything there?' he asks, on his knees, inspecting the stain.

Gareth bends down to look. 'Not a drop,' he says. 'I think you're safe this time.'

*

At parents' evening, a mother tells him he looks younger than she expected. He smiles when she says this. Other mothers compliment him on the wall displays, on how beautiful the class looks. They say that their children

34

talk about him all the time. He looks at the class drawers – at each child's name he has written out in neat, round-edged letters – and tells the parents that their children are wonderful. And for the most part, he means it – he is constantly surprised by the way the children respond to things. Maybe he should try to react to life the way they do. But he suspects that he is *already* too childish, that this is the part of him that annoys his wife. Each night, when he hears her car pulling into the drive, he switches off the Xbox and pretends he's been doing work all evening. He should become an adult, he thinks. He should start doing adult things. He looks at his arms – *they are too thin, too scrawny to belong to a man.*

He has the idea of a dinner party. She's reluctant ('Can't we just do something alone?'), but he talks her round to it. He invites two of the other young teachers, Sara and Rhian. They turn up, both with bottles of wine. He cooks fish. Was it stupid not to have invited anyone else? He can see that his wife is finding the dinner difficult. They are all talking about teaching and the kids and other teachers, and she's just having to nod along. He squeezes her thigh under the table and she strokes his hand, then softly pushes it away.

Sara's the same age as him, but she is held together well, her hair neat, her features clear and intentional. He feels like a mess beside her. It was stupid to invite her, he thinks. She's telling jokes, making fun of the kids in her class and she's starting to dominate the evening. She keeps cutting across him and Rhian, and he thinks his wife is laughing too much at the things Sara's saying.

They are all drunk now and sitting on the couch, on the floor. Sara says they should play truth or dare. Rhian says that's a bad idea. He reckons so too, but he doesn't want to show himself up in front of them all.

'When did you lose your virginity?' Sara asks after a few rounds.

'I was twelve,' he says before anyone else can respond. And then there's silence. It isn't true – his wife knows this; he lost his virginity to her – but he's glad to finally shut Sara up.

That night he climbs on top of his wife and when they fuck it seems powered by the events of earlier. He comes inside her and it feels good. Afterwards, they lie entwined, her head on his chest, him arm resting around her neck. The streetlight outside glows orange through the curtains. He gently strokes her arm. 'I really do love you,' he says. 'I know,' she says. 'I really do love you too.'

He decides to start going to the gym after school. He likes it. He likes seeing his wife at the sports centre. He likes the dank light, the feeling that he's initiated into a private world there, that he knows more about the mechanics of the place than others. It reminds him of after-school classes, of being in the assembly hall with the night melting purple through the windows. He goes to the gym two, three times a week. Swimming, treadmills, rowing machines. He develops muscles in places he never knew possible. The simple act of walking suddenly feels easier than before, as if his legs are springing him forward. This must be how his wife feels all the time, he thinks. He's happy. They book a holiday for May half-term. Portugal.

He's sleeping better now, but on the nights he can't sleep, he heads downstairs, to the living room, and spends hours on the internet or playing FIFA on the Xbox. Sometimes, he goes to Google Street View, looks up his street, and tries to get as close as possible to his own house. He'll move through the street, zooming in on all the other semi-detached houses, all the other small lawns and hedges. He moves through the streets, but he never sees the castle.

In the kitchen, when he makes himself a glass of squash or a cup of tea, the windows are dark with the night outside, and he sees a fuzzy reflection of himself in the stillness. One night he notices that the silver clock on the kitchen wall has stopped. He climbs onto the counter-top and changes the battery.

*

The mornings are dark when he wakes. But since starting at the gym he feels more capable, more energetic. He is no longer bothered by the frost on the wheelie bins, backlit orange with the hum of morning streetlamps. He doesn't feel beaten by the front lawns in the street, glistening with shards of ice that look like tiny bits of glass. It's always cold in the car at first, but he just wipes the inside of the windscreen with his sleeve, turns on the heater, and drives to work.

He's teaching the kids about the Normans. Caerphilly Castle is only a ten-minute walk from the school, so he takes them for a tour. He explains how Gilbert de Clare built the castle when the French invaded Wales. It's the second largest in Europe, he tells them. Touch the stones, he says, they're over seven hundred years old. One of the kids asks about the Green Lady. So he tells his class about Gilbert de Clare's wife, Alice, and how she fell in love with a Welsh prince. When her husband found out about the affair, he had the prince hanged. And when Alice heard the news, she dropped dead from shock and a broken heart. From that day on, her ghost, dressed in green for Gilbert's envy, haunted the castle. She still haunts it now, he says. She's waiting for the prince to come back. The boys try to look cool about it, they make ghost noises and creep up on the girls, and tap them on their shoulders, but he can tell they're all scared. He takes them into one of the towers and explains that the stairwells curve to the right to make it harder for intruders to swing their swords. They reach the top of the tower and one of the girls, Elen, a little thing with blonde hair, looks pale. 'Are you okay?' he asks, and then he sees the flow of blood running from her nose. He hands her a tissue from his pocket, tells her to tilt her head, to hold her nose tight. It's just a nosebleed, he says, there's nothing to worry about. He hugs her.

In the second week of February, there's heavy snow. School is cancelled for two days, but he still gets up early. He makes breakfast for his wife, and they watch *The Little Mermaid* in bed. On the second day, they bring the duvet out to the couch and watch *Pocahontas*. He never saw these films as a kid, but in the last ten years he must have watched them at least ten times. On the couch, as they lie there, he strokes her neck, but he's afraid to kiss it, he's afraid that if he does she'll ask him to stop.

The first day back after the snow, Elen stays behind when the class empties for dinner hour. She walks up to his desk, and hands him a folded A4 sheet of purple paper. In red felt-tip pen, faint on the purple, she has drawn a big wobbly love-heart, and written inside: '*your the besst. i luv u.*'

'For Valentines,' she says, studying his eyes.

He tells her it's very sweet, but she should give the card to someone else in the class. She starts to cry, and he puts a hand on her shoulder.

'It's a lovely card,' he says, 'but if my wife saw it she'd be very jealous.'

She pushes his hand away. 'Then don't show her.'

The snow melts and March arrives. On St David's Day, the kids come in dressed like children from the past: top hats and check woollen skirts for the girls, and Dai caps and shorts for the boys, with leeks and daffodils pinned to their Welsh rugby jerseys. During dinner hour, when they're playing football on the yard, one of the boys rips the felt leek off another's jumper, and they both end up crying. It takes the remainder of the break to get the two sides of the story, to calm them both and shake hands. By the time it's over, he has missed dinner. In the afternoon, after the St David's Day assembly, the headmaster calls him in and says he wants to elect him for a fast-track headmaster's course.

'Are you sure?' he says. 'I'm only twenty-seven.'

'You know how it goes,' the headmaster says, smiling. 'A man in a primary school is gold dust.'

They're sitting in the headmaster's office, and he's nodding now, and rubbing the back of his leg, feeling the new definition of his thigh. He feels his head tightening with hunger.

'Well,' he says. 'If it means I get to dress as badly you, I'm in.'

'Good man,' the headmaster says, laughing. 'The course starts in April.'

When he gets home, there's a cellophaned plate of Welsh Cakes on the kitchen table, and a note from his wife: '*Mam made these for us. I got called in so I'll see you later. Love you.*' He eats four of the cakes in a row. Then he goes to the bathroom and throws up in the toilet. He flushes the chain, but bits of cake still float in the water. He flushes again, and this time it all disappears. He gets changed, takes an apple from the fruit bowl, and heads to the gym.

It's getting lighter in the evenings now. And driving to the sports centre, he remembers those evening walks to her house when he was seventeen. Stopped at the lights by the castle, he remembers the day he was accepted to study illustration at art college. How he walked all the way from his house to hers, how Caerphilly was bathed in sponge-gold light, and the stillness of spring seemed to flow through him, made him think that everything was possible.

Over the last six weeks, he has worked up a personal best on the exercise bike: 10K in 21 minutes, 43 seconds. He pedals quickly and rhythmically, feeling his quads tighten and push as his legs rotate through the motions. Mounted on the wall, Sky News plays with the sound muted and the subtitles on. When the Education Minister talks about the mess-up in the GCSE marking, and the lack of top grades, the subtitles say: 'There were certainly fewer grey days'.

He's going at a good pace now and he imagines the fat burning off around his waist. Where does it go, he thinks, all that fat?

As he reaches the last kilometre, he's near to beating his personal best. He goes to stand on the pedals, to push himself through the last eight hundred metres. He knows he can do it. With six hundred to go, he realises it's close, so he pushes one bit harder and then there's a snapping noise in his leg. He falls off the bike and onto the floor. People look on, until a woman gets off a treadmill to help. Are you okay? she says, but he is clutching his leg, and crying – something he hasn't done since he was seven, the day his parents took him to McDonald's to tell him his father was leaving.

His wife is called from the pool, and together with another man from the gym, she helps carry him into the car. He remembers his father leaving now, how he didn't cry until the journey home. When his mother leaned over and asked if he was okay, he said he was only upset because he'd left his Batmobile in McDonald's.

A week of helping him in and out of the bath. A week of helping him put on his socks in the mornings. In class, it hurts to stand for long periods of time, so he starts teaching from a sitting position. He watches the kids as they work, thirty heads faced down, thirty hands writing away. He looks out at the empty schoolyard, and pictures it filling with children at break time. As a child, he spent whole days staring out this window.

At home he asks his wife to bring the swivel chair down from the office, and with his good leg he pulls himself around the place.

'Nice wheels,' she says when he rolls past her in the living room.

In town, he notices how many other people have limps

and deformed walks. It's like a word he's just learned and suddenly sees everywhere. Twice a week he attends physio after school. He wears shorts under his chinos, and all day he wonders if the kids can see the waistband through the fabric of his trousers. The physio is attractive, and before each session he worries about getting erections with her. After the fourth session, he decides to cancel the appointments. 'It's nothing personal,' he tells the receptionist on his way out, 'I've just found one closer to home.'

In the evenings, when his wife is at the pool, he watches porn on his phone. He masturbates two or three times a night – in his bedroom, in the kitchen, in the bathroom. It's guilt-making, but he continues anyway. After a few weeks, he is bored of stock studio porn and begins to seek real sex – sex between couples, filmed on beds in actual bedrooms. Sometimes it'll take him twenty or thirty videos to find the right one. He'll mindlessly skip through images of women choking on cocks or being pumped upside down, until he finds something tender. He searches for 'beautiful' and 'shy' and 'gentle' and it leads him invariably to teen porn, to girls of seventeen and eighteen years old. He wonders if he'll always be attracted to girls of this age.

Weeks limp by. Every day his wife asks how the hamstring is doing. Good, he says, it'll be perfect by Portugal. But he has stopped doing the morning stretches, has begun to find the tightness and the dull ache kind of soothing.

When she's out at the pool, he takes long baths. She can't stand them herself, she says it's just bathing in your own crap. But growing up there was no shower in his house, and he only ever had baths. He even washes his hair in there now, taking a plastic jug from the kitchen. It was his father who taught him how to wash his hair. It's one of the last things he remembers him doing before he left. His father told him to put some shampoo – the size of a two-pence coin – onto the palm of his hand and run it through his hair. Then, he said, he was to rinse until the hair was squeaky between forefinger and thumb. And tonight, as he squeezes a squirt of shampoo, he visualises the two-pence coin in the centre of his hand.

He takes his wife's tweezers from the bathroom cabinet and inspects himself in the mirror. He finds a hair just above his eyebrow – a thin white one, spooling from his forehead. He plucks it out. He wipes the tweezers and returns them to the cabinet. Wearing just a towel, he walks downstairs slowly, one step at a time – it still hurts to go any faster – and goes to the kitchen, and out to the garden. He looks across to Caerphilly mountain. Clouds slide across from left to right, and he can hear a plane overhead. It brings back a memory of an August afternoon when he was eight or nine. How he lay on the warm pavement outside the house, listening to the sound of passing planes, of lawns being mowed, of cars being washed, and savouring how it had felt that morning, the first to wake, watching cartoons on the couch in the living room as his mother slept on, above him in her bed.

He thinks now of the months after his father left, all the times he played football on his own – using the garage door as a goal, all the times he lay on the road, his leg under a car trying to scoop out a ball that got caught between the chassis and the ground. And all these days have merged into one long summer's day, and every year he remembers less and less.

His sleep gets worse again. He can't seem to rest. He is tired and his thoughts keep fidgeting. His wife is already asleep, sprawled over the duvet, her face a deflated ball, a trail of spit from her mouth to the pillow. He dresses himself in a T-shirt off the floor, goes downstairs to the living room, and plays FIFA on the Xbox. He starts an FA Cup campaign with Man Utd. He wins the first game 2–0. He wins the second 3–1. After two hours, with his eyes feeling hard, he makes it through to the final. It's 3.30 a.m. and he'll leave for school in four hours.

He goes to the kitchen to make himself a drink. The house is quiet, just the sound of the kettle gearing. He puts a tea bag into his Man Utd mug. The fridge hums, like a laptop waking up from idle. He takes out a pint of milk, places it beside the cup. The kettle's ready. He pours the water, adds the milk, spoons in two sugars and stirs. He's never won the FA Cup on FIFA before.

He sits with his back against the leather couch, and drinks the tea slowly, agonising over which players to pick.

He goes 1–0 up, then 2–0, but the computer comes back: 2–1, 2–2. The match goes to extra time. He's wired. The controller is warm in his hands, and his fingers ache from all the rubbing against plastic. If he thought about it, he wouldn't even know what his hands are doing on the controller now. They're on autopilot, like the controller is an extension of him. He's through on goal, but hits the post. The other team has a good chance, but it goes wide. He shoots, but it's tipped over the bar by the keeper. And now their team is through on goal, their striker is rounding *his* keeper, putting the ball into an empty net. It's 3–2 to the computer. And before he has time to launch another attack, the whistle goes, he's lost the game.

He puts the controller down beside him, and starts punching the floor. He punches until his knuckles are bleeding, he punches until there's blood on the fibres of the thick cream carpet.

Then he goes to the kitchen, takes a bottle of washing-up liquid and a rag, and comes back to the living room. His knuckles sting raw, and he gets on his knees and scrubs the small stain, but it only makes it worse, it only spreads the stain a thin salmon-pink. He thinks about scissors, cutting the fibres out so his wife won't see it in the morning. He thinks of moving the couch forward, but he knows she'll notice. He googles 'removing blood from carpet', and learns to blot the stain with a clean tea towel, not to scrub. He blots and he blots until the stain lifts, until the white tea towel absorbs the blood. He does this for twenty minutes, and by the end he has no idea whether he can see the stain or not.

He needs a wee now. He doesn't want to wake his wife with the sound, so he takes his trainers from the front hall, goes to the kitchen and puts them on at the back door. He quietly slides the French doors open. It's nippy out, and the garden light comes on. He goes around to the drain under the kitchen window, gently pulls down the front of his pyjama trousers, and pisses.

While he goes, feeling his bladder release and empty, he puts his face up to the window and looks into the kitchen. The long fluorescent strip-light illuminates everything, and he can see the stack of cups, the silver clock, and the little chrome cooker. From outside, it seems like he's looking at someone else's home.

Steam rises from the drain. He shakes off the last drips and pulls up his trousers. He goes inside, and takes his shoes off at the door. He moves to the sink, runs the hot tap, and squirts some washing-up liquid – the size of a two-pence coin, too much really – onto the palm of his hand. He rubs his hands together and rinses them. The water flows into the grey plastic basin in the sink and bubbles begin to form. When his mother first taught him to use bubble bath he thought she was stupid for keeping the hot water running.

'But won't the water melt the bubbles?' he asked.

'Just watch,' she said, and the bath slowly filled with soft white foam.

He leaves the tap to run, and stares out the window. But when the night's as dark as this, the window becomes a black mirror, reflecting the kitchen. He normally doesn't think much of it, but tonight it seems odd to look out at the garden, and see the contents of the kitchen projected on it all. He knows by memory where everything should be, so it's strange to see the row of cups where the clothes line should be, the eerie-looking strip-light where the tree should be, and then, finally, to see his image looking back at him from the kitchen window – but it seeming as if he's still outside, as if he's standing in the garden looking in.

FUGUE

'Drown me! Roast me! Hang me! Do whatever you please,' said Brer Rabbit. 'Only please, Brer Fox, please don't throw me into the briar patch.'

On the way back from Cardiff, your father asks questions about Edinburgh and Tim. You answer vaguely, and look out the window as the landmarks of approaching home draw near. You haven't been back in a year, and you'd forgotten that these places – Castell Coch, the roundabout at Nantgarw, the Total garage on the dual carriageway – even exist.

Side-on, your father's eyes seem like two swollen capital Ds – glassy and unreal. And while he rambles on about the garden and next door's dog, you're sat there in the passenger seat, thinking *am I really this man's daughter?* He looks like your father, but it's been so long, you can't be sure.

You never realised your house had its own smell until the first time you came back after being away, and it hits you again as you enter the hall and drop your bag into your room. You're sitting at the table now, a Chinese takeaway doled out onto plates. The Christmas tree is where it is every year, three feet to the right of the telly. It makes the room feel smaller than it actually is.

'You got a nice one this year,' you say.

'It's alright, isn't it?' your mother says. 'Thirty-eight pounds, though. Can you believe that?'

The tree sags, leans a little to the right. The skin under your mother's eyes is sagging, too.

'Thirty-eight pounds?' you say, and feel your own voice strain. 'That's robbery. You'll need therapy for that.'

You tell your parents about Tim's new job, how he's working as the sound man on a documentary series about a housing estate in Glasgow. There are three episodes, you say, each one focused on a different family. A very different job to the others he's done. He has to get the sound right first time. Can't really ask a woman whose son has died of a heroin overdose to redo the bit about finding his body because of 'noise interference'.

Your parents are the picture of attentiveness, nodding as you speak.

'And the paper?' your mother asks. 'You still enjoying it?'

'Yeah,' you say, and set your cutlery down on the plate. 'All good.'

Your life in Edinburgh is like the tiny tag of skin that hangs under your left armpit – you sometimes want to share your fears about it, but know you can't face the diagnosis, or rather, you can't face the embarrassment of having to admit you let it linger for so long.

Your father says he saw Rhian in town yesterday. You tell him you're meeting up with her tomorrow, for Christmas Eve drinks.

'Glad to hear it,' your mother says, and she asks if you want a bit of caterpillar cake. Her accent sounds odd, exaggerated, the kind you'd get on a tourism advert or a poorly done BBC Wales sitcom.

'I think I'll pass,' you say. 'I ate a load of crap on the train.'

Your father takes the plates out to the kitchen, and you hear the rattle-thud as he sets them down beside the sink. While the taps run, your mother tells you about your aunt getting trapped in a lift. She was stuck in there for forty-five minutes. Debenhams gave her a £100 gift voucher as an apology.

Your mother says, 'So we can all guess where she'll be buying her presents this year.'

When you were seven, you spent the whole winter thinking your parents weren't your parents. You were afraid to confront them about it, so you told your aunt. They were imposters, you said. They were aliens who were inhabiting your parents' bodies. You expected them to rip off their skin any minute, to peel back their faces, reveal a shrunken skull, and go *ha-ha, tricked you!*

A different family member might have suggested counselling, but your aunt told you not to tell anyone.

She gave you a set of Brer Rabbit books, and said to read them whenever you felt afraid. But you were so horrified by the Tar Baby story that you began to fear tar. You crossed roads to avoid pavement repairs, you left the room when your parents smoked. Unbidden, the image of tar comes to your mind now.

You yawn, palm your eyes.

'Tired?' your mother asks, and you nod slowly. Your father comes back in and plumps himself on the couch. You watch as he takes a Chinese cracker from the polythene bag, watch as his jaws masticate. He sets the crackers on the couch and scratches his neck, and you think again about those nights you lay awake, convinced your parents might eat you.

'Yeah, I'm knackered,' you say. 'Travelling's no good for the body. My average speed today was probably eighty miles an hour.'

*

You get into bed, take your laptop out, and scroll through page after page on Facebook, drinking the wine you picked up at Crewe station. You text Tim and tell him you miss him – more out of muscle memory than genuine longing.

On Facebook, you look up all the people you used to go to school with. You never really do this in Edinburgh – you're more concerned with all your friends there – but this drawing back to school people always happens whenever you come home. And here they are: slowly – and quickly – turning into adults. You wonder if they ever look at your pictures, if they ever wonder what you're up to now.

When your battery dies, you can't be bothered to get the charger from your suitcase, so you pour yourself a cup of wine and look through the long-abandoned clothes in your wardrobe. There's a pair of flattering jeans in there somewhere. You asked your mother to post them up to Edinburgh, but she never could find them. The wine tastes metallic and you imagine bits of the foil have fallen into the bottle. But it doesn't stop you drinking. You sit cross-legged, take mouthfuls of wine, and keep searching through the pile of crap at the bottom of your wardrobe.

No jeans, but in a green Dr Martens shoebox you find three old diaries from when you were fourteen and fifteen. You sit on the floor, your back against the bed, your wine beside you. You read.

You thought you'd find 'embarrassing' declarations of love to dreadful guys – something you could ironically joke about with friends, but instead the diaries document two years of crippling self-consciousness, and what you interpret now as a depression that seems heavier than the usual teenage angst. The diaries are only ten years old, but already you can't remember the fifteen-year-old who seems so unhappy in these pages.

You finish the wine before the diaries, and begin to feel uneasy. You sit up on the bed and look out the window, out at next-door's garden, at the kennel at the back – the view you had until you were eighteen. You can't believe you forgot the way it felt to lie in this bed, the way it felt to look out this window. You look again at the photos that you Pritt-Sticked into these old diaries – photos of you and red-cheeked friends on the double-decker school bus, wearing tiny fat ties.

The house is so small that everyone can hear everything everyone is doing at every moment – especially bathroom noises. So, at 12 a.m., when you need to be sick from the wine, you go out into the street. You hope to throw up into the bushes at the bottom of the road. But you only make it as far as the postbox. You throw up all over the pavement.

*

Next morning, hung over, you're watching *Santa Claus: The Movie* on the couch when your mother calls.

'Up, are you?' she says.

'No,' you say.

'Will you check if we've got any butter in the fridge? I'm in Asda's with your father and he says we've plenty already.'

You carry the phone into the kitchen.

'There's marge here,' you say, kneeling down, looking in the fridge.

'It's butter I want to know about,' she says.

'Well, I can't see any.'

'Maybe it's under the ham,' she says. You look. She's right.

'Yeah,' you say, closing the fridge door. 'There's butter here.' You look out the kitchen window, out at the frost-covered garden shed. Your father built the shed for your sixth birthday. But in the last few years it's become your mother's 'Place of Tranquillity' – she goes there to get away from him.

'How much left?' she says.

'I don't know,' you say.

'Will you check, then, please? My darling, wonderful daughter?'

You try not to sigh down the phone.

The tub is mainly empty – just odd slivers with tiny bits of burnt toast, and serrated swathes around the edge from where your father wipes his knife. You picture the butter being squeezed through his veins and thickening his waist, his neck. You think of liposuction and that moment in *Fight Club* when they steal all the bags of human fat.

'There's not much left, no.'

'Ha! I was right, Ben,' your mother says, and you picture your father in the refrigerated aisle, wearing his black Berghaus fleece, his plump hand resting on the trolley. 'Okay,' your mother says. 'That's all I wanted to know. Are you out tonight?'

'We'll see,' you say.

And this house, these rooms, this phone, these voices – you know they should mean more to you, but they don't. It's like the opposite of déjà vu.

*

Outside, in the weak afternoon light, your hands feel brittle with the cold. You think – once again – that you really should see a doctor about your circulation. But in Edinburgh you still haven't registered with the GP. You don't know why you've put it off for so long. It's not intentional – nothing you do ever feels fully intentional – but the doctor just seems like too serious a task to sort out on your own.

When you reach the postbox you see your sick from last night. You can just about make out the scraps of chicken, the rice, the peas, and the blood-red wine, all frozen under a thick skin of ice. It disgusts you, but you're a little intrigued by it too. You study the vomit and think: *homesick; ice-sick-les.*

The bridge over the train track is icy, so you walk carefully, holding onto the rail as you make your way down the other side. Slowly and steadily, you walk past the bus station.

The shop across the road from New Look is boarded

up. Posters for a travelling circus are pasted to the boards. To the best of your knowledge, a travelling circus has never passed through Caerphilly, but whenever a shop closes down, a poster advertising one always appears.

Decorations and festive mannequins fill the other shop windows, but it all feels muted, as if someone has turned the colour down.

You call Rhian to see if she's around. She doesn't answer. You try the other girls, but no one answers at all.

You walk to Tesco. The place has the feel of Christmas Eve – there's something dozy and antsy about it, as if the staff are sleepwalking and waiting for the place to close. Though this Tesco has always felt that way. Wherever you are in the store you can pretty much always hear the checkout beeps – like little pips on a heart monitor.

You watch the girl on checkout 3, with the reindeer-ear headband, stare at the gelled-hair boy on checkout 2 as he flirts with the girl packing bags. There's love and longing and heartbreak in that look.

A box of Ferrero Rocher for your father. A bottle of Shloer for your mum. In the queue, a woman hacks up a God-awful cough. You think she looks like one of those 'If You're Working Class, Smoking Will Give You Cancer' adverts. Her bones shake with each cough. It makes your lungs ache, thinking of all that tar searing the hairs, the cilia. You think of the Tar Baby again, of

Brer Fox rolling a creature out of tar, trapping Brer Rabbit in the middle of the street.

At home, you internet for two hours until your eyes feel dull. You half-read articles on the *Guardian*, and look at photos of yourself and your old school friends again. When they went away to university, they all came back that first Christmas overweight – the drink, your parents said. And now there are no photos from that year: everyone has de-tagged and deleted them.

You read an article about life extension, and learn that people actually *do* cryogenically freeze themselves – it's not just something from the movies. There's a problem, though: the skin and bones are cracking at the low temperatures.

'But we shouldn't worry,' one of the scientists in the article says. 'Whatever technology is capable of reviving a frozen human will be more than able to mend cracked tissue.'

He explains about the tiny microphones they keep in the freezers, that monitor for the sound of skin and bones splintering.

Between looking at photos of school and uni, you refresh Gmail at least forty-eight times. You don't know why, but you just have this feeling that an email is coming your way, from someone somewhere who wants to give you money, or a holiday, or something; maybe even a message saying how well you've been doing, how well you've done, and *yes, yes you are right, you are special; that nagging feeling you have at the back of the neck, the one that itches when you're asked to do pointless, life-wasting tasks at work – like 'research' on small businesses in Fife – that itch has been my way of saying you're meant for something else, something important, and don't you worry, your time will come.*

You go the front room and install yourself on the couch. You eat half a tube of Pringles. Then throw the tube across the room onto your mother's chair – to stop yourself from eating the rest. When the adverts come on, you go to the chair, take the tube, tip a handful out and chomp them like one big Pringle sandwich.

This isn't depression, you think. This is eating.

*

You're asleep on the couch when your father's voice wakes you.

'Easy now,' he's saying, and you can hear your mother going *ah ah ah*. Out in the hall, you watch your mother leaning on your father. She's hopping on one foot.

'What the hell—?'

'She slipped on the ice,' your father says.

Your mother looks at you, she looks in pain.

'When did it happen?' you say.

'Just now,' she says. 'I got out the car to post a card, and there was a patch of ice right next to the postbox.

I didn't see it.' She grimaces, and her face looks awful, rubbery. *Ice-sick-les,* you think.

'I reckon she'll live,' your father says, easing off her coat and hanging it on the banister.

She pulls another pained face. 'It bloody hurts, though.'

Your father hands you the car keys. He asks you to bring in the shopping while he helps your mother into her chair. The car boot is filled to the brim with Asda carrier bags, which makes you feel oddly guilty. These big supermarket trips are something you haven't done in years. The scale and drama used to be part of the weekly family experience. But in Edinburgh you live day to day, just buying bits when you need them.

Your mother is in her chair now, her left leg propped up on a cushion on a dining-table chair, a bag of peas and a check tea towel wrapped around her ankle.

'What are you doing?' you ask.

'Rice,' she says.

'What?'

'Your father just googled it on his phone. Rest, ice, compression and . . . God, I can't remember what the E stands for.'

'Elevation!' he shouts from the kitchen.

'Right,' you say. 'How is it, though? Does it hurt?'

'It feels as if something's trying to climb out of it,' she says, and she bends forward to take off the tea towel, to show you her ankle. It's swollen purple like old women's legs in documentaries about DVT and negligent care homes.

'Bad, isn't it?' she says.

'Shit, yeah,' you say.

Your father emerges from the kitchen. 'Do you know what swelling actually is?' he says. Neither you nor your mum answers. 'Internal bleeding,' he says.

'Thanks for that,' your mother says. 'Really needed to hear that.'

'I just thought it was interesting,' he says.

*

Your father once asked: 'What are you running away from?'

You told him you weren't running away from anything.

He said: 'You are, you're running away from reality.'

For your father, reality means living in South Wales, working a job you hate.

You didn't say: Our generation is different to yours! We expect job satisfaction, and even that's not enough! We want meaning!

You didn't say: Struggling in a city seems more romantic and noble than struggling in Caerphilly!

You said: 'I'm trying to build a life for myself.'

'I see,' he said.

*

You know Rhian only answered because your landline came up as no-number. The conversation drips and drabs, and you awkward her into inviting you to the new Wetherspoons. She says none of the girls will be staying out too late tonight.

'No bother,' you say. 'It'd just be good to see you.'

When you get out the bath – a towel wrapped around you – your father is standing on the landing.

'Glad you're out,' he says. 'I'm busting for the loo.'

'All yours,' you say, gesturing towards the bathroom.

'What happened to your arm?'

'What?'

'Those scars on your arm there.' He moves forward, runs his hand over the skin below your shoulder. He says the scars look like cigarette burns. He peers closer. 'What happened? They're perfectly round.'

'I've had them years,' you say. 'They're from blood tests in college.'

'Oh right,' he says. 'Anyway, out my way.'

You don't tell him you got so skint that you sold your skin to a cosmetic company. Nor do you say that they only gave you £120 for it, that the money only covered your council tax.

'Anything else you want to interrogate?' you say, and you lift your arms as if being frisked at airport security.

He closes the bathroom door and shouts: 'I demand to have my piss in peace.'

*

You get changed, dry your hair, do your make-up, then Skype with Tim. He asks you to show him your tits, so you oblige. He tells you all the things he wants to do to you when you're back in Edinburgh. You tell him that sounds nice.

'I miss you,' he says.

'I miss you too,' you say.

You go downstairs, shout 'bye' from the hall but no one answers. You walk to the living room and you picture – for one head-buzzing moment – your parents as aliens, catching them with their human skin shed on the floor.

You open the door.

Your mother is asleep in her chair, your father zonked out on the couch. As quiet as a mouse in socks, you leave the house.

*

It's 8 p.m. now; dark, the air cold and icy on your cheeks, the roads slippy underfoot. The queue for the Uphill is absurd, going all the way up the street. The bouncer says it's taking thirty minutes for people to get in, and everyone is complaining that it's too arctic to wait any longer. Most of the queue guys have probably been drinking since noon and they're already pissed. You call Rhian to see if she's inside, but you get no answer.

Traffic moves slowly up and down the hill. As cars approach, the guys beside you go *ooooh*. . . and hold it, building the pitch until the car is passing them. If the driver is female they let out a *yay*. And if the driver is male, the guys *boo*. One of the boys seems anxious, and he keeps checking his phone, his wallet, his driver's license. As you move along the queue, the car game is transformed into *yaying* and *booing* the people who leave the pub.

When you're finally in, you do a circuit but don't find anyone you know. The place seems filled with girls with auburn tans and guys with massive arms wearing Christmas jumpers. You go to the bar, which is four and five people deep, and after ten minutes of avoiding eye contact with queue-people, you order a large glass of wine. The barmaid asks to see ID. You hand over your passport. She studies the photo, then returns it, shaking her head.

'Twenty-five?' she says. 'Well, it'll catch up with you eventually.'

'What will?' you shout over the noise.

'Time,' she says. Though she might have actually said wine. It's loud. It's hard to tell.

Taking a place in the corner of the bar, you text Rhian, then scroll through your contacts, looking for someone or something else. You consider texting Tim, but figure he'll be bored out of his head at home with his parents. He might just see the text as an invitation to call. Or to enter into a series of text messages about missing you, or all the ways his parents are dreadful people.

You're reading through your Sent Items when you feel someone behind you, at your shoulder. It's Dale Edwards, whom you spent the best part of Year 9 fancying. The last time you saw him and his mates, a few years back, they all looked old and bloated. But he's looking alright now.

'On your own again, are you?' he says, taking a casual swig of his pint. 'What'd you do this time?'

'How's it going?' you say. 'I'm just waiting on Rhian and the girls.'

He says he didn't realise you were still friends with that lot, and then he asks you to come over to him and the boys – *only until Rhian shows up*, he says. You weigh it up, then follow him to an alcove in the corner. The walls are made from the same plastic as the Frankenstein's monster mask you had as a kid. And the plastic has been painted black and designed to be lumpy – it's been designed to look like coal.

The boys – except for Dale – are massive. They look as if they've been inflated with a foot pump.

'Been working out, have they?' you say to Dale.

'On the 'roids,' he says. 'You watch, there'll be fighting by twelve o clock – 'roid rage!'

They get in Sambucas, and drink Jägerbombs until Marc Jones is spewing. Dale goes to the bar, and Andy Hywel, a boy you once gave head to in Rhian's shed, tries to get you to do shots with him.

'With our arms linked!' he says. You think: Andy, you held my head down until my neck hurt, and you didn't tell me you were going to come.

'Nah, I'm alright,' you say.

Nine years later, and you still remember the smell of mildew and the whiff of dog on the carpet you were kneeling on.

Dale comes back with a glass of wine for you, and before you've taken your third sip, he's finished his drink and insists it's your round.

You do Jägerbombs and talk shit about Rhian and the girls. Dale does impressions of Rhian, and says *fuck them* because *they're* the ones who're stuck-up. You drink four more glasses of wine, a pint of cider, and a shot of cherry-flavoured tequila.

*

When it's closing time and the bouncers kick everyone out, a shoal of people gather outside the doors. You're at the edges of the group, drunk-hungry and demanding food.

'Charcoal Grill?' Dale says.

'Won't it be closed?' you say.

'Course not,' he says. 'They're Muslims. They hate Christmas.'

Dale has traded in this kind of 'ironic' racism ever since he watched *The Office* in 2004 – back then you found it funny.

'Actually,' you say. 'I'm pretty sure—'

'*Actually*,' Dale goes, sounding all posh. 'Whatever. Turkish then. Anyway, they'll be open. I bet you a tenner.'

The rest of the boys head to what's now called the Irish Tymes, and you and Dale sway to Charcoal Grill. You slip on the ice but Dale grabs you before you fall, and insists on walking arm in arm *for safety reasons*. You know the arm-linking is flirting, but you consider it harmless. You'd hate it if Tim linked arms with another girl, but this is different, you think – this is you.

Down Cardiff Road you both go, the grit under your feet sounding like heavy-duty sandpaper. When you get to Charcoal Grill, it's closed.

'Probably plotting,' Dale says, his hands and face against the door, examining the inside. He turns around. 'You'll wake up tomorrow, having a great time cos it's Christmas, and you're there eating your turkey, Queen's Speech on the telly, and your nan's falling asleep and then BOOM! Caerphilly Castle blows up. Terrorist attack. A thousand years of history wiped out.'

'Eight hundred—'

'And Tesco covered in rubble. And the ducks dead. And—'

His phone rings. He answers.

'Where you to?' he says. 'Really? Yeah, yeah, alright. What's the number again?' He does a funny shuffle on the spot, intending to amuse you. 'Right,' he says. 'Nice one. I'll see you in five then.'

He eyes you up and down. 'Fancy a house party?'

'It's Christmas Eve,' you say.

'So what? It's not like Christmas is good anymore.'

'Is it far, though?' you say. 'I'm freezing.'

'A four-minute walk,' he says. 'Come on, it'll be a good laugh.'

You think: why the fuck not.

He takes your arm again, and you walk slowly up the hill, walking in the road to avoid the worst of the ice. Plastic stars hang from lampposts and glisten dully. You pass the taxi rank and Dale nods to a driver sitting idle in his car. The guy looks at you, then says to Dale, 'Happy Christmas, pal.'

You pass the Tymes, and look through the window, wondering if Rhian and the girls are actually in there. But the pub is rammed, the windows blushed with condensation. When you turn the corner, someone shouts, 'Give her one from me, Dale.'

'No idea who that was,' Dale says.

'Lovely,' you say.

Past the bus station, down to Bartlett Street, where the houses seem to all have Christmas trees in the windows, glowing warm light. There's a noise, a *doof-hum*, coming from a house farther down the road.

'That'll be the party,' he says.

When you arrive, Dale knocks then realises the door is unlocked. Inside, you're greeted by Huw James, Dale's old best mate from school. He looks fat in the face, with some very dodgy facial hair going on.

He high-fives Dale, then seeing you he shouts: 'Bethan Jones!' and picks you up, his arms wrapped around your waist. 'Happy fucking Christmas!!'

You can't tell if he's shouting because he's happy or because of the noise. The house vibrates with the sound of the party.

You ask him where to put your coat and he shouts *fuck knows*, then tells you to throw it in the room on the right because no one's in there.

You enter and Dale follows. You feel the wall for the light switch, and Dale giggles as your hand flails. When the light comes on, you see a bundle of wrapped presents on the floor. In the corner there are coats and jackets piled three feet high, and beside them leather couches, armchairs, dining-room chairs, and a coffee table, stacked like a quarter-complete game of Tetris. And finally, there, in the middle of the room – a baby, sleeping in a cot.

'Oh my God,' you say.

'Baby Jesus,' Huw says, popping his head between yours and Dale's. 'He's having a birthday nap.'

'Whose is it?' you whisper.

'Kath's,' he says. 'Don't worry, though, her girls are in bed.'

You switch off the light, quietly close the door, and slowly back away.

*

The living room is in such a state that you're almost sobered by it. It's filled with people – men, women, teenagers – and it's just one big expanse of mess. John Lennon's 'Happy Xmas' is playing, but the noise of chatter is so loud you can only hear the music now and then, like a phone call cutting in and out. From the imprints in the carpet, you can see where the table and couches once were. On the wall are studio photos of two little girls, looking airbrushed on fluffy white blankets. And a few other family shots, with backgrounds as white as cleaned-out yoghurt pots.

And that's when you recognise the coughing woman from Tesco. She's standing there, a can of Strongbow in her hand. She gives Dale a kiss on the cheek. 'My big boy's turned up,' she says.

'Howsitgoing, Kath?' he says. And then he turns to you and gestures towards the woman. 'This is whose party it is.'

You're still holding your coat, and you smile – the kind of awkward smile you usually reserve for dog walkers.

The woman's skin is pale and thin, like semi-skimmed milk. She has heavy bags under her eyes.

'Thanks for having us,' you say.

'Glad to have you here,' she says. 'The more the merrier.'

Dale leads you through to the kitchen. The sink is full of dishes and baking trays and saucepans. On the draining board there are empty and crushed cans of Dutch Gold and Stella, fag ash dusting the ring pulls. The party smells stale. It feels as if it took place last night.

Dale eyes some food on the table.

'Aye aye,' he says, squeezing past a girl who looks barely fifteen.

'Aye aye, chips and pie,' says Huw, emerging from behind the fridge, and jumping on Dale's back.

'Mini pizza, actually,' says Dale, shrugging him off. He removes the cling film, then puts a tiny pizza, the diameter of a mug, to his mouth. 'Want some?'

'Are you sure these are for us?' you say.

'Course,' he says, taking a bite. 'It's a party.'

You take two mini pizzas, and Dale picks up another two, before pulling the cling film back over the empty plate.

'Fair play,' says Dale. 'They've put on a good spread. Iceland's finest, this is.'

'How do you know Kath?' you say, scratching the itch at the base of your chin.

Dale points in Huw's direction – he's punching the fridge in an effort to impress the fifteen-year-old-looking girl. 'She works at the Kings,' Dale says. 'Kath does, I mean.'

'Right,' you say.

'But her boyfriend walked out a few months back. And Huw's been trying to bang her ever since.'

'She's a bit old for him, isn't she?' you say, and again you find yourself scratching your chin. It feels like something is breaking out under the skin, a spot or a small tumour or something.

'Huw likes them old,' Dale says. 'And he loves kids, too, you know?'

You look at Huw teaching the girl how to throw a punch. He has his fists in the air, bobbing and swinging like a boxing coach.

'Oh, you know what I mean,' says Dale. 'He's not a paedo or nothing.'

Dale rinses out a cup in the sink, and you watch him swirl his finger in the shallows, then half-fill it with the rosé he found beside the kettle. He hands you the cup, then drinks from the bottle.

You lay your coat over a chair, and you want to tell Dale that it feels so familiar now, that all those teen house parties and nights under dark skies are coming back to you, that it feels like nothing has changed. But you know you can't say it. That saying it would be to suggest this place hasn't progressed, hasn't moved on like you have. And that would just be an obnoxious thing to say.

'D'you know I've got my own photography business now?' he says.

'Really?' you say. 'What kind of photos do you do?'

'Just weddings and portraits and shit like that.'

He whips his phone from his trouser pocket and snaps a picture. He turns away from you and studies the photo.

'Lovely,' he says. 'One for the wank-bank, that is.'

'What? Me fully clothed?' you say. 'You must be desperate.'

He laughs. 'Well . . .'

'Keep dreaming,' you say, putting your cup down on the side. 'Let me have a look then.'

'Nuh-uh,' he says. And you grab for the phone. He wriggles away from you, and you move closer, try to pin him against the sink. He puts his arms high in the air – the phone in one hand, the wine in the other – and you and him are face to face now. You look at him, at his nose, his lips.

A kerfuffle behind you then. It's Kath. She's next to the table, holding up the empty mini pizzas plate.

'They was part of the dinner for tomorrow,' she says.

You take a step away from Dale, and he goes: 'What?'

'The pizzas,' Kath says. 'They was meant for tomorrow.'

'Oh shit,' you say. 'I'm so sorry, we had no idea.'

'Why d'you think I put cling film on them?' Kath says.

You shake your head.

'Well, what am I gonna do now then?' she says.

You're both quiet. The kitchen has gone quiet, people are looking at you.

'I'm so sorry,' you say.

'You can be sorry all you want, love. But what am I gonna give my kids tomorrow?'

Dale goes, 'Can we give you some money?'

Kath licks her teeth, has a think. 'Aye,' she says. 'Yeah, give me some money for them.'

Dale puts his hands into his pockets and pulls out a load of change. In your own jeans, you feel what's either a receipt or a five-pound note. You take it out. A five-pound note.

You hand it to Dale. He gives it to Kath.

'Will eight quid do?'

'It'll haftoo, won't it?' she says.

'We're so sorry,' you say.

'Don't worry about it now,' Kath says. 'It's too late, innit? But next time, keep your fucking hands to yourself, alright?'

She leaves for the living room, and Dale whispers to you, 'Two pounds per mini pizza. She's made a right profit on that.'

*

You're both sat on the landing, backs against the wall, jeaned legs dangling through the banisters. You're at the state of intoxication where every thought seems immensely profound. Every now and then, you save a draft of a text with an observation you want to remember in the morning. You haven't replied to Tim's last three texts, but you don't particularly care.

Dale's been 'accidentally' brushing his leg against your leg, and his arm against your arm. And though you don't really know where it'll lead, you're kind of tingling from it. You're thawing.

'You have very sad eyes,' he says, deliberately stroking your arm now. 'Why you so sad?'

'The sad eyes line,' you say. 'That's a classic.'

'You do, though,' he says. He moves his other hand into your lap, begins stroking the fabric of the jeans. You watch his hand strum the zip.

'I'm not sad,' you say. 'I'm . . . I feel . . .'

You try to find the word you want. *Confused* isn't enough, and *discombobulated* is too long, not precise enough. The word *fissured* comes to mind, but you're not sure what it means.

'I feel . . . fissured,' you say.

Dale nods, and slowly cups your crotch, his thumb resting on your zip.

'Know what I mean?' you say.

He caresses through your jeans now. 'I'm not sure,' he says.

'Like,' you say, 'do you ever feel . . . like . . . I mean, do you ever feel like you're not you?'

'You're getting too deep for me now,' he says, and he smiles, caresses you harder.

'Don't you, though?' you say. You're aware of his hand, but it feels as though it's not really happening, or that you have no control – it's as if you're watching the scene from outside of yourself.

'Come to the bathroom with me?' he says.

'What for?'

He looks down at his crotch, then yours.

'I can't,' you say.

'Why not?' he says.

'Boyfriend.'

'Don't worry,' he says. 'I won't tell anyone.' He digs deeper into you now, rubbing the heel of his hand against you.

'No,' you say.

'Oh, come on,' he says. 'You know you want to.'

'Stop it,' you say, but he only grinds harder.

You grab his hand and push it away.

'I'm popping to the loo,' you say. 'I'll be back in a minute.'

'Should I—?'

'On my own.'

You go to the bathroom and lock the door. Tim once pointed out that it's a film cliché for a character to go into a bathroom to 'pull themselves together' – and that is exactly what you want to do now. But when you look in the mirror, the reflection isn't familiar. You can't pick out a single feature that belongs to you.

You sit on the toilet and try to picture Tim, try to imagine his voice – not saying any words as such, but its sound, its timbre – but you can't, and you realise he no longer feels like someone real to you. A flash of something awful then – your friends and family hanging from hooks in an anonymous white cupboard.

You stand up and that's when you see the massive frozen turkey on a silver tray, defrosting in the bath. You kneel down, put your head very close to the carcass. You think: that's why Kath bought the pizzas – the fucking turkey won't defrost.

Pink and goose-pimpled, the turkey looks like a deformed baby. You rest an ear to it, but you can't hear a thing: no sounds of bones cracking or flaking. Then you think: when you get home, you'll take a trowel from your mother's shed and hack at the sick-ice by the post-box, hack until the threads of chicken, rice and peas are freed from the ice. It'll be a symbolic act of penance.

You sidle quietly out the bathroom, but Dale has gone. You think a crazy thought: maybe he was never there to begin with. You're heading for the stairs when you hear a murmur, a heaving coming from one of the bedrooms. You imagine it all: the sound coming from the wardrobe. You'll slide back the door, and all your friends and family will be naked, hanging from hooks like dead cows. Your mother's eyes open, looking out at you. Her skin pale, her lashes dusted with ice.

You follow the sound. The door is half-open. You peep round. Kath is there, kneeling on the floor, her head and arms buried deep in a pile of clothes. She's making a wailing noise.

'You okay?'

She tells you to fuck off, her voice muffled by the clothes.

'I'm sorry I'm sorry,' you say, and close the door, the hinges squealing. You stand outside for a moment, consider the best way to leave. There's singing from downstairs now, a gang of people belting out Slade.

You think: if this were an episode of *EastEnders*, a man – in a cross-cut scene – would be discovering that his child isn't his, that his wife has been having an affair. As he throws a photo at a wall, Slade's 'Merry Xmas Everybody' would play over it all.

The door creaks slowly open. Kath peers out

'I'm sorry, love,' she says, palming her eyes.

'No, no,' you say. 'I'll go. I shouldn't have—'

'Come in,' she says.

'It's fine.'

'Please,' she says. 'Please come in.'

You enter the room, trying to be small, unintrusive. On the floor, in front of the wardrobe, there's a pile of men's shirts, jumpers and jeans. A minute ago, Kath's head was deep among them.

'I'm sorry about the mini pizzas,' you say.

'What, love?'

'We shouldn't have taken them,' you say. 'I said to Dale—'

'Oh, it don't matter.'

She asks you to sit on the bed beside her. She gestures at the empty spot. You can't say no.

'How old are you, love?' she says. She looks tired, her face drooping like there's too much skin.

'Twenty-five,' you say.

'You're so young,' she says. 'Have you got a boyfriend?'

You nod.

'That's good,' she says, and she takes your hand. 'Cos the older you get, all the people you meet have so much shit going on. And you've got your own shit too. It just piles up. And then you've got your shit, and they've got their shit, and well, it's all just shit.'

You don't know what to say. Your life hasn't prepared you for this. You look past her, towards the bedside table. It's covered with mugs and glasses, scrunched-up tissues, and glass bottles of tablets. The duvet on the bed has no cover.

'Oh God,' Kath says. 'I can't believe you saw me cry.'

'Don't be . . .' you say. 'You alright?'

She tightens her grip on your hand. 'The house is in such a state,' she says.

'It's okay,' you say. 'I'll help you tidy up.'

'You're very sweet,' she says, stroking your fingers. 'Very pretty, too.'

You watch her yellow fingers move over yours. The skin on the back of her hand is wrinkled brown, and a gold ring seems loose on her wedding finger. She looks at you now, her cheeks puffy from the crying.

'God,' she says, 'I just shouldn't have invited people over. It was such a stupid idea.'

'It'll be okay,' you say, and Kath runs her tongue across her teeth again, like she did downstairs.

'Oh, I dunno any more,' she says, her voice breaking, her head dropping. You imagine her opening up now, explaining how badly she's been doing since her boyfriend left. How she wanted this Christmas to finally be a good one, how she bought the turkey two days ago but it wouldn't defrost. She just wanted her kids to have a real Christmas dinner – just this once.

You go to put your arm around Kath, to tell her that everything will be okay. But she pushes you away, and puts a hand to each of her own cheeks. She starts massaging then, rubbing the flesh, and slowly, very slowly, lifts the skin from beneath her chin, and begins peeling the skin over her nose, and her eyes, and peeling, peeling, until her face has gone, until all that is left is bone – white hard bone.

STRANGE TRAFFIC

Jimmy Hughes asked Mrs Morgan out every week for three months before she finally gave in and said he could accompany her to the Big Cheese festival on Saturday, but that it wasn't a date, and that she had to be back by five because she was babysitting her great-granddaughter. He found the message Thursday morning. It had been pushed through his letterbox, written in claw-like handwriting on a scrap of lined blue paper. In the queue at Glanmor's, on the bench by the castle, and under the fluorescent purple hue of Morrisons' toilets, Jimmy read the note over and over again. That evening, he boasted about the date to the guys at the Cons Club, and at last orders Stan the Bread planted a box of Durex on Jimmy's table, and said in very serious tones: 'In case you get lucky, Jimbo. You can never be too careful.'

Pocketing the condoms, Jimmy said, 'Well, I hope these buggers come with instructions.'

Dilys Edwards was perched on a bar stool at the fruit machine and listening to every word. She dropped a twenty-pence coin into the slot, and hollered, 'As if

Hughes could get his plunger up. It'd be like fitting a glove on a baby slug.'

The men laughed, and Jimmy punched the air and held his arm erect. 'My cock is like that dog they put in space,' he said, pumping his arm. 'It's still up there and it's never coming down.'

Dilys thumped a button on the machine, and a succession of coins kerchinged into the payline gulley. 'Oh Jimmy,' she said. 'Oh poor, delusional Jimmy.'

At home, Jimmy read the letter again before settling to bed. It was a hot July night and his thoughts were fireworks, exploding all kinds of colours in the dark. He planned the outfit he'd wear, and the jokes and stories he'd tell. He pictured himself and Mrs Morgan among the festival's stalls, looking at handmade trinkets, and eating ice cream on a bench. Yes, he was seventy-eight, and yes, he was twice a widower, but he figured he was in good enough shape to last another ten years, and where was the point in going lonely all that time?

He opened the window to let in some air, but all that entered was a rush of street noise – drunks, arguments, music – and a strew of moths that whizzed and darted across the walls and ceiling, their faint whir enough to startle him when he was close to sleep. Lying awake in his musty sheets, he thought of the last time he saw Mrs Morgan. She had been in Tesco, talking about desserts to the skeletal boy who stocked the bakery aisle. She told him she had a sweet tooth, and that she kept a supply of raspberry doughnuts in the house, going so far – he heard her tell the boy – as to keep an emergency bag of doughnuts in the freezer. Jimmy was diabetic and wondered if his disease might somehow count against him. I must keep her off the topic, he thought. I mustn't let the conversation turn to cakes.

Friday was a slow fudge of a day. Jimmy woke late and woke tired. He took his retinue of tablets and under-boiled an egg. The runny yolk dripped onto his best tie as he spooned it into his mouth. By noon the yolk had hardened into a crusty yellow scab which he picked at with a fingernail. The egg-scab lifted but left a shadow, and Jimmy made a mental note to put a wash on that evening. It usually took him two days to face the washing machine, but tonight he'd get it done. He was sure of that.

He headed out for his daily stroll, and when he passed Mrs Morgan's house the white lace curtains were drawn but didn't fully meet. All he glimpsed, in one brief moment, was a blue ironing board heaped with clothes, and beside it an empty chair.

Down to town he went, pausing for a break at the bench by the castle. Last week he had noticed seagulls sneaking into the moat and swimming around, pretending to be ducks. And now they were at it again, moving there in the water, like cars in a bus lane, and taking the town's good-willed bread-givers for fools. He convinced a young mother and her little daughter Natalie – who seemed to be on some kind of lead – to throw their bread onto the path instead.

'Mark my words,' Jimmy said. 'When that bird comes out of there he'll have a nose as pointy as a Cornetto.'

The child tossed a slice onto the stone path, and the bobbing figure that had been eddying up against the rim of the moat jumped up and out, grabbed the bread in its seagullian beak, and flew up to the fence that enclosed the Court House pub.

The mother laughed. 'That's ridiculous,' she said. 'They shouldn't be allowed to get away with that.'

'Credit where it's due, though,' Jimmy said. 'They really do look like ducks when their legs are hid.'

He coughed then, a deep whooping cough that he caught in his fist. When the cough subsided, he fiddled in his top pocket, took out a Fisherman's Friend and offered one to the mother. She declined and said they were too strong for her, that they always took her head off.

'My own daughter says the same,' Jimmy said, popping one into his mouth.

The mother smiled, and said they'd better be off now. She walked away, with her daughter a few yards ahead, attached by the umbilical cable. Jimmy kicked a stone into the moat and his knee twinged.

Across the water, a convoy of enormous trucks streamed down the road. Jimmy watched as they pulled up near the park, with all the disassembled carnival rides strapped to their backs. He'd seen it all before, but it still excited him. He knew that men in blue overalls and hi-vis jackets would spend the day and night assembling and building the rides, ready for tomorrow.

He came every year to the festival, and every year the festival got better and the crowds got worse. There was no perfect weather for it, he thought – a bit of sun and there'd be too many people, a bit of rain and the place became a grey smudge, the grass slippy and dangerous, the footbridge a mess of squelched mud and torn greenery. Three years ago – when he came with June, his second wife – it had rained all weekend and he'd slipped on the bridge and bruised his hip.

But sun had been forecast for tomorrow, and he'd be spending the day with Mrs Morgan. And though she said it wasn't a date, Jimmy knew she was only just saying that.

When he arrived at the library, Angela asked what the hold-up had been. Since June had died, Jimmy had come there every Monday and Friday, and was usually through the doors at eleven sharp.

'Ah, I dunno where the day's gone,' he said, extracting a DVD from his pocket. 'The hours seems to have gotten away from me.'

'I've had whole years like that,' Angela said. 'This one any good?'

'Aye,' he said. 'Not as good as the first two, but I do like Tom Cruise.'

She checked in the DVD with the hand scanner. The scanner beep-beeped and she put the film to one side. 'Before I forget,' she said, 'I've got something for you here.'

She bent down, and fiddled beneath the counter. Jimmy could hear a rustling, and a moment later Angela rose bearing a small bouquet of carnations.

'Flowers,' he said.

'For you,' she said. 'Well, for Mary's . . . Been ten years, hasn't it?'

He looked past Angela for a moment, as if the answer was on the Big Cheese poster behind her.

'*Duw*. Ten years. So it has,' he said. He smoothed his egg-stained tie, then touched the petals. 'They're lovely flowers, fair play.'

'Do you want them now? Or will I give them to you —?'

'When I'm leaving,' he said, and he put his hands into his trouser pockets, and jangled some loose change. He pulled out a handkerchief, dabbed his brow, and said half to Angela and half to no one, 'It's bloody warm out there.'

'It always is for the Big Cheese,' she replied.

'Aye.'

'You going this year?' she asked. He thought of mentioning Mrs Morgan, but it didn't seem right, not now with the carnations – red, pink and white – there on the dark wood countertop.

'Might do,' he said. 'Aye, I might do indeed.'

He went to the computer and opened his email. He had just one: from his daughter, saying she didn't have time to write a full message, but that she hoped he was okay. She was thinking of him – and Mam, of course – and she'd be sure to call tomorrow. *You'll be in at 10 a.m. your time, right?*

The Cons was quiet when Jimmy arrived that afternoon. The last day of school, most of the club's usual folk were rambling around Caerphilly, savouring the town before it got taken over for the summer. On Monday, the shopping centre, the benches, and Caerphilly's narrow side-lanes would be overrun by mouthy kids who roamed the streets like they owned the place. And in what had become an annual ritual, Stan the Bread had gone to Trecenydd Snooker Club to enjoy a teenager-less afternoon of play. Jimmy wasn't fussed about snooker so he'd given it a miss. And that's how he found himself in the Cons, drinking a cup of tea, eating a Glanmor's ham-salad roll, and being berated by Dilys Edwards.

'You shouldn't be bothering a younger woman,' she said.

'Oh for God's sake, Dilys,' he said. 'She's seventy-three.'

'Exactly,' Dilys said, gripping her lemonade and black. 'You're making yourself look like an utter twat.'

'Am I, now?' he said.

'Yes, you are,' she said, and she took a long shaky swig of her drink. 'Mary. Then June. You've already seen off two women, and now you want to finish a third?'

'Woah now—'

'Well, God rest both their souls. That goes without saying.'

Jimmy smoothed his tie. 'Yes, indeed,' he said.

'Don't you think of them, though?'

'Of course,' he said.

'And you still feel it's okay to cavort like you do?'

'Listen,' he said. He was about to once again share his views on living in the past, but stopped himself before he spoke. He just hadn't the energy to go into it all. 'Look,' he said, 'I can't help if women find me irresistible.'

'Ha!' said Dilys. 'That's right. Hundreds of women across the town poisoning their husbands and smothering them with pillows, and all so they can shack up with Jimmy Hughes.'

'Lowest form of humour that is,' Jimmy said.

'And you're the lowest form of human,' she replied.

'Now now,' he said, clutching his chest. 'That hurts. You've mortally wounded me there.'

'Just listen,' Dilys said. 'That woman met her Don at fourteen. They were married before she was nineteen and she's never set eyes – not even a *glance* – at another man. Can't you just leave her alone? She's only going with you out of pity.'

Jimmy rested his roll on the table. 'She tell you that?'

'Course not,' Dilys said. 'When would I have spoken to that bloody woman? It's plain as day, though. She lives for her family – she spends half her days running after those kids, and she loves it. She's happy as a dolphin as she is.'

'But she didn't tell you this herself?'

'No,' Dilys answered.

Jimmy reached for his ham-salad roll again. 'There we go then,' he said. 'You are speculating without a valid source.' He took a bite of the roll and chewed with an immodest grin. He chewed some more, then swallowed. 'Barkeep!' he shouted. 'A blackcurrant for the lady. But dun bother with the lemonade. She's—'

'You're a twat,' Dilys said. She gathered her things and stood up. 'You were a twat when you were a boy, you're twat right now, and tomorrow you're going to be crowned King Twat of Caerphilly.'

He watched Dilys leave the bar, and sipped his tea.

'She must be off her tablets,' he later told a drunken Stan the Bread. 'That's all I can think.'

'Aye,' said Stan. 'Either that or she's jealous.' Stan was sitting at the fruit machine, mashing the buttons with his fist.

'You what?' Jimmy said. Stan punched a button and stared intently at the machine. He seemed stuck, on pause.

'Stan?' said Jimmy. 'You alive, mate?'

Stan put twenty pence into the slot, and took a swig of his pint. 'Aye, I bet Dilys is jealous,' he said. 'Thinking about it, her Bernie died a year before Don Morgan. Dil probably thought she was next in line for your services.'

Jimmy laughed, but it came out like a sigh.

'You know,' Stan said, his eyes on the fruit machine, 'I still can't believe Bernie's dead.'

'I know,' Jimmy said, loosening his tie a touch. The air was close in the club, hot.

'Can't believe Don's dead, either,' Stan said. 'Always thought he'd live to a hundred.'

'Me too,' Jimmy said. His head felt steamed now, and he ran his hand through his hair. Had they left the heating on or something?

'Same with Mary, though,' Stan said. 'I always thought—'

'Yes,' said Jimmy. And his heart scrunched a little in its cage.

'And June,' said Stan. 'God, I'm still not over that one myself. Falling down the stairs and—'

'For God's sake, Stanley.'

'What?' said Stan, and he finally turned from the machine.

'They're all dead,' Jimmy said. 'I get it.'

'Sorry, Jimbo?'

'Oh, nothing, Stan,' Jimmy said, rubbing his eyes. 'Long day.'

Stan got up off his chair and settled on the couch beside Jimmy. The fruit machine's lights illuminated and faded, then lit up again.

'Ah, I'm sorry, Jimbo. If you ask me, you've always had the right idea, though. No good looking back. Speaking of which—' and Stan gestured at the carnations next to Jimmy, 'these pretty flowers – they for tomorrow's date?'

*

Jimmy filled a saucepan with water, dropped in the carnations, and placed the pan on his dining table. It was 8 p.m. This time tomorrow his date with Mrs Morgan would be over, and he'd know for certain where things – where he and she – actually stood. The thought made him nauseous.

From the pile of clothes that had bonfired their way to the height of his bed, he took a pair of underpants, his best pair of trousers, and his favourite shirt, and then carried them down to the kitchen. He almost forgot his egg-stained tie, but something triggered the first time he closed the washing-machine door. De-noosed, he opened the door again and flung in the tie. A light wash, yes, but he couldn't be bothered to fetch more clothes. The sooner he got it done, the sooner he could put it all out on the line.

He turned on the TV and settled in his chair. The walk to the library and back, the flowers and the ten-year anniversary, the arguments with Dilys and Stan, and all the thinking about tomorrow had left him sieved and tired.

His hair was thicker in the dream. He dreamt he was talking to Don Morgan at the Cons, the two of them sitting in the dark, in the corner of the bar, with moths flying at Jimmy's head. He tried to bat them away, but still they came – and moths, dead moths, nestled now between the thick strands of his hair. He pulled them out, their wings crumbling between his fingers, and he kept finding more and more as he tore at his scalp, dragging out the moths and flicking them under the table. He felt for a switch on the wall. If I can turn on the light, they'll go to that, he thought. They only want the light.

Don didn't seem to notice the moths. He slowly sipped his pint and spoke about the afterlife, talking calmly. He said it was all lovely but the only problem was for those who'd remarried. Don had met a man who was living happily with his first wife, but when the train came in and brought in the second wife, all hell broke loose. And it begged the question: with which wife should a man spend his second life?

*

Morning light snuck through the curtains, and Jimmy woke in his chair with the phone ringing. He pretended he'd been up all morning, and when his daughter asked if he visited the grave yesterday, he said to her, 'What sort of question is that?' She apologised, and said sorry for not sending a card. He told her not to be silly, and scratched his head, as if the moths were still in there.

Then he drew the curtains back and was greeted by a perfect cloudless sky.

'I have to go,' he said. 'I've um . . . I've left an egg on to boil. Can we—?'

'I'm off out in a bit,' she said. 'But maybe I can call you again tomorrow? For a proper chat?'

He fingered the curtains carefully. If he got the angle right, he could just about see into Mrs Morgan's window. 'Aye, that'll work nicely,' he said, peering out at the street. 'I'll speak to you then.'

In the note, Mrs Morgan had said she'd meet him outside the optician's at 1 p.m. She was having her hair done at Marsh's in the morning, and he wasn't to come knocking or making a show of himself at her front door.

It was half ten now, so he had less than three hours to dry his clothes.

The trousers, shirt and tie were heavy as he lifted them out of the washing machine and slung them over his drooping garden line. Taking slow paces, he came in, went upstairs and ran a bath.

'Time for my ablutions,' he said aloud.

He got in, he soaked.

He bathed, he dried.

Out his front window, the sky was blue, but out back it had become grey and dark, and was threatening rain. In his dressing gown, he shouldered the back door open. The lawn was overgrown with clumpy weeds, and the long grass tickled his shins. He heaved the shirt, trousers and tie into the house, and felt a sweat collecting on his back, the blood rising in his cheeks. He now had less than two hours to dry the clothes and meet Mrs Morgan. And yes he was already hot – and yes he was loathe to do it in summer – but he turned on the central heating, and threw the clothes onto the radiator.

The radiators clanked, and he slouched on his chair and dabbed at his forehead with his handkerchief. He felt a heat in his groin, and opened his gown. His stomach, his balls and penis drooped in front of him. His shoulders sloped, and his arms hung loosely at his side.

'Oh bloody hell,' he said aloud, to himself and the empty house.

For breakfast, he ate an over-boiled egg. Then he massaged his trousers on the radiator – they were still damp, but the shirt was drying nicely.

He paced and he sat, and he stood and he paced, and he sat and he waited.

Out the windows – front and back – the sky was now blueing. And he imagined himself and Mrs Morgan walking side by side down Cardiff Road, past Super-Click and Lloyds Bank, and heading to the castle. He wouldn't offer his arm until the walk home. She might be a little tired then. She'd be thankful for the extra support up the hill.

He twitched his curtains and peeked across at Mrs Morgan's place. Her daughter's green Nissan was parked outside the house. He wondered: why the hell is her daughter here?

He caught sight of himself in the window, and decided to shave.

So he climbed the stairs again, applied the razor, and as he put on the aftershave the St Martin's Church bell tolled for twelve o'clock.

In his chair he tried to read his Helen Mirren biography. But the words weren't going in.

He patted down the trousers, the shirt and the tie – and they were finally dry. So he switched off the central heating and removed his dressing gown. Then it dawned on him: his underpants were still in the washing machine.

He could wear a dirty pair – but wearing a dirty pair always itched his arse, and, well, what if he did get lucky later?

He lifted the heavy-wet pants from the machine, took a plate from the cupboard, and dropped them onto the plate. He set the microwave for three minutes on medium-high. He stood beside it – he'd heard you shouldn't stand directly in front of the machine – and he stopped the cycle every thirty seconds to check. When he opened the door, steam rose from the damp grey pants.

*

His underpants were toasty, and scorched along the hems, but they were mostly dry. And Jimmy felt good as he walked down Cardiff Road with Mrs Morgan by his side. She was wearing a little purple around the eyes, and a purple cardigan too. It couldn't be a coincidence, he thought. She'd made the effort just for him.

'Lovely day for it now, isn't it?' he said as they passed Greggs.

'It is,' she said.

There had been talk that Cardiff Road would be pedestrianised for the day, and here it was: no cars, no buses, nothing but people. Jimmy watched them go: the groups of families, the kids on fathers' shoulders, the children pushing their own prams, the little girls in sun hats, and also the gangs of topless boys. He watched as everyone spilled over the road and pavements, walking up and down and across – never looking at the lights – and harrying around the town like such strange traffic.

'You getting on well?' he asked Mrs Morgan.

'I am,' she said.

He'd expected her to ask him the same, but she only looked to the other side of the road, to the charity shops and the hairdressers. Stan the Bread stood outside the florists, grinning and waving at the two of them.

'Odd man, isn't he?' she said.

'The oddest,' Jimmy said, and he palmed down the back of his hair. 'By the way, did I see your daughter at yours earlier?'

Mrs Morgan looked at Jimmy, her features locked in a way he couldn't read. 'Spying on me now, are we?'

'No, no,' he said, 'Just thought I saw her car.'

Mrs Morgan laughed. 'You always were a nosy sod.'

Jimmy turned his head and smiled.

'She was visiting for washing duties,' Mrs Morgan added. 'I appear to have become the family laundrette.'

The festival heaved with bodies, and kids ran around as if their legs powered the sun. Mrs Morgan smiled at all the babies in prams and the children in medieval costumes.

'It's something special, isn't it?' she said.

'It really is,' he said. And for the first time in a long time, Jimmy found himself enjoying being among the crowds. Caerphilly, he noticed – as he always noticed on this far side of the castle – lay in a basin, and mountains and hills surrounded the town 360 degrees. Some days it felt as if they were closing in on him, like the seagulls going after the bread, but today the hills seemed to promise space, a vastness and a calmness, even when things were crazy-mad down here.

He looked forward to the festival itself now, and not just being there with Mrs Morgan. He couldn't wait to see the falconry show and the re-enactments. He remembered the one year he'd seen a great sword fight between two men in costume, and then only an hour later he'd seen the same men, in full medieval garb, wandering through Tesco, holding a bottle of cider and a sandwich each. The image had stayed with him – the men walking bare-faced among the present, like a horse and cart going the wrong direction up Cardiff Road.

'Don used to love all this,' Mrs Morgan said. 'He really loved the castle.'

'He was a good man,' Jimmy said.

'He was always annoyed about the lack of cheese though. Why call it the Big Cheese unless there's a lot of cheese, he'd say. He loved his cheese.'

'Cheese is good,' Jimmy said, and he then remembered that he'd forgotten to take his tablets at breakfast.

They approached a wooden clothes stall where Mrs Morgan inspected the garments. She became enamoured with a woollen cardigan. She felt it between her fingers, and rubbed the fabric against her cheek. The woman at the stall told her the clothes were all handmade, that it was a family-run business. Mrs Morgan smiled and began caressing the other items: little children's hats, dresses and jumpers. Jimmy stroked a blue scarf, but he was still thinking about his diabetes tablets, how he'd left them beside the kettle on the kitchen counter.

'That one's eighteen pounds,' the woman told Mrs Morgan.

'My my,' said Mrs Morgan, and she held the white cardigan aloft, as if inspecting it under a light. 'I think it's worth it, though. It'll look lovely on Elen.' She riffled through her bag then, pulled out pens and a cheque book, but could only find a ten-pound note. Jimmy coolly took a twenty from his pocket and handed it to the woman behind the stall. Mrs Morgan only noticed when she heard the money box clink shut and Jimmy pocketed the change.

'I could have sworn I had a twenty in here,' she said, shaking her head.

He told her not to worry, and she stressed that she would pay him back as soon as she got home. They walked on, past the burger vans and the candyfloss stalls, and when they reached the food tent Mrs Morgan said, 'Tell me, what's your favourite cake?'

Jimmy protested and insisted he was fine, that she didn't need to buy him anything. But she became so adamant, he couldn't say no. He told her he liked the look of the Danish pastries, so she bought one of those, and two chocolate brownies for herself. And then she found a foam mat on the grass for them to settle on.

'I'm having mine now,' she said, unwrapping the cling film from her brownie. 'You sure you won't have yours too?'

'I might have a little nibble,' he said, and he opened the brown bag and removed the pastry. He took a small nervous bite and imagined his arm cut open with a knife, and a bag of Silver Spoon sugar being poured straight into his bloodstream.

'Fair dos,' Mrs Morgan said, swallowing her first bite. 'This brownie is bloody lovely.'

Jimmy sat back and told himself not to worry. As he'd missed his tablets, a bit of sugar would do him good. He took another bite of the pastry, and looked at the castle, bathed in glorious doughy light.

'God bless the Vikings,' he said. 'They do make cracking pastries.'

Mrs Morgan laughed. 'Is there anything you'd like to see here today then?'

'Other than your good self?' he said, and he tilted his head in imitation of a child seeking approval.

'Hughes,' she said. 'You're insufferable.'

'Can't blame a man,' he said, and he took another bite of his pastry, picturing the sugar rushing through his blood. 'Actually, I'd love to have a good look at the falconry,' he said. 'Those hawks are amazing. They could spot a pastry from a hundred feet.'

'I could smell one from two hundred,' she said.

'A hawk?' he said.

'No, you idiot. A pastry!'

They both laughed, and a spaceship-sounding ringtone emanated from Mrs Morgan's handbag. Jimmy repeated the joke quietly – '*I could smell a hawk from two hundred feet*' – and Mrs Morgan answered her phone.

'Never!' she said. 'Are you? . . . Really? Where to? . . . Yeah, of course! Come over, I'm just eating a cake. Outside the food tent I am.'

Jimmy watched her jaw and her mouth as she spoke. A few brownie crumbs tickled her lips, and he was sure she was wearing lipstick. And her hair, its tight curls, seemed preened and measured. Ah, there was no doubting it, she really was the most beautiful woman in Caerphilly.

'That was Ben, my grandson,' she said, returning her phone to her bag. 'He's down here with little Elen.'

'Oh right,' Jimmy said. 'Very good.'

'They'll be over in a minute now.'

He pulled a few blades of grass and held them in his hand. 'What?' he said. 'Over here?'

'Yes,' she said.

He dropped the grass onto the mat. 'Very good,' he said. 'Very good.'

Mrs Morgan took another bite of her brownie, and her eyes grinned then darted past and beyond Jimmy.

'They train them from when they're really young,' he said.

'Sorry?' she said.

'The hawks,' Jimmy said. 'You can send them off and they'll fly for miles but they'll always find their way back.'

'Ah, right.'

'It's amazing really,' he said. 'You'll see when we head over now. The man sends the bird flying halfway across Caerphilly and then he blows a whistle, and *whooooosh*, the hawk is back in a flash and swoops down onto his hand. I dunno how they train them to do that.'

Mrs Morgan nodded along, and then suddenly rose. 'Ah, there she is!'

'Nanny-nan!' a little blonde girl called, and came bounding over. 'Nanny-nan, Nanny-nan! We're going to McDonald's!'

Ben, the girl's father, followed behind. He was wearing a Welsh rugby top, and had a massive Winnie the Pooh tucked under his arm. He had a young face, but Jimmy noticed his hair was already receding.

'All this food here,' Ben said, 'and she wants to go to bloody McDonald's. Can you believe it?'

'I can and I do,' Mrs Morgan said. 'And I've got a bit of brownie here for afters, too.'

Ben smiled at Jimmy. 'Alright mate?'

'Very good, thank you,' Jimmy said.

'So is Nanny-nan coming, Dad?' the girl said.

'Ah, you don't have to, Nan,' Ben said. 'I know it's hardly your favourite place in the world.'

Jimmy brushed his mouth with the back of his hand. He could feel shards of pastry clinging to the sweat on his lip.

Ben added, 'It's totally up to you, Nan.'

A seagull cawed, and Jimmy's blood rattled. He looked at Mrs Morgan, at her hair, her nose, at her fingers that gripped the brownie bag, and he imagined all the workings of her organs now, all the things going on inside to keep her standing there, breathing.

'Well,' she said finally, patting Elen on the head, 'how could I say no to my great-granddaughter?'

Jimmy shrunk and felt his heart wither.

The little girl looked at him like he was some figure she'd learned at school, whose name she couldn't quite remember. Mrs Morgan was happy as a dolphin, he thought. She didn't need him. King Twat, indeed.

'Do you wanna come too?' said Ben. 'Sorry, I dun know your name.'

Jimmy's blood sugar was draining to his feet, he was sure he could feel it. 'Nah, I'm alright,' he said.

'You'd be welcome,' said Mrs Morgan.

'It's okay,' Jimmy said. 'I have to be heading back now anyway.'

'You sure?' she said.

Jimmy worried his tie, curled its end around a finger. 'My meds,' he said. 'I forgot to take them this morning. And the daughter's calling in a while. In Australia, she is, so . . .'

'Oh right,' said Mrs Morgan. Elen pulled at her father's arm, and Mrs Morgan went, 'Well, if you're sure.'

'Yes, yes,' Jimmy said. 'I've got a lot to be getting on with.'

'Well, okay then,' said Mrs Morgan. 'I guess I'll see you when I do.'

Jimmy nodded slowly. 'Aye,' he said. 'I guess you will.'

Elen pulled at her father's arm again, and made pleading noises. 'Right,' said Mrs Morgan, 'let's go to McRubbish before Elen tears her daddy's arm off.'

Ben and Elen gave him a wave, and Jimmy bobbed a little, his head bent. He gave back a small wave – not even looking at Mrs Morgan – then turned and walked away.

He didn't know where he was going. He didn't want to see the falconry now, it seemed pointless. But something, some heavy current, was rising inside his chest, and he felt he had to go somewhere, anywhere, before it welled any higher. He walked along the path for a while, but there was so little space that people kept brushing against him. There was a woman on stilts, dressed in green, and children walked under her legs and tugged at her long, long trousers. She's going to fall, Jimmy thought. Any moment now, she'll fall to the ground. Beyond her, he could see the rides, the roller coasters and the Ferris wheels. The noise of the screaming made him think of sports days, playgrounds, and the years he worked as a bus driver on the school run.

He got off the path, and found himself walking on the grass, down towards the moat. The banking was steep, and it hurt his legs to keep balanced. It was so hot, and his head felt tight, and the thing inside his chest rose and caught in his throat now, made his mouth dry. Mary, June, Mrs Morgan, they've all left, he thought. They all keep leaving. He moved his way down the banking towards the water. I'll feed the ducks, he thought, or the seagulls or whatever they bloody are.

He was throwing bits of his pastry into the moat when, above him on the path, a man and a woman in medieval tunics strode past, the man's sword clanking against his leather belt. The woman wore a long skirt, and carried a wicker basket looped around her arm, a loaf of bread peeking out. Jimmy stopped and stood there, near the water and the gathering seagulls, and watched the knight and his maiden cross the bridge, growing smaller as they travelled deeper into the castle grounds.

He threw a piece of his pastry further into the water then, for the smaller duck that hung back. And he was about to toss in the final piece when he heard his name being called.

'Well, that's a waste of a good pastry,' the voice said. The voice belonged to her, to Mrs Morgan.

'But . . . you'd left,' he said. 'You'd gone.'

'Ah, it always starts with McDonald's,' she said, moving towards him. 'But it usually ends with me doing the ironing, the washing, or looking after the kids for the bloody night. I'm seeing them later anyway.'

He was holding the last bit of pastry in his hand. 'But you'd left,' he said. 'I watched you go.'

'Well, I'm here,' she said, offering her arm and smiling. 'Now come on, the hawk show's starting.'

I.

When the police tried to arrest me I couldn't tell them my name.

'He's resisting disclosure,' said the one with the Elvis quiff. His bald colleague, an ex-army type, shook his head.

'Don't play the tough guy with me, *mate*,' he said. 'Tell us your shitting name.'

I insisted I had a stammer. I tried to spell out the letters but this only angered them. I was singled out as a troublemaker and left on my own in the back of the car.

My friends were lined against the front garden wall, three sports bags and a fully inflated yellow dinghy on the pavement in front of them. Gareth, boxer shorts over his jeans, looked perturbed. But Gareth always looked perturbed. His father was obsessed with germs and made him change his bedding every day.

Larry, meanwhile, looked cocky. With his parka done up tight around his neck, he kept laughing, and I could see this was annoying Gareth. Boxer shorts aside, Gareth was serious. Gareth wore glasses.

But Larry remained cocky, and he pointed across the road, towards the house where the phone call had apparently been made.

'I wouldn't trust them with a muffin,' he said.

And we all understood the reference. A year earlier, the bald one had been at Queen Street shopping centre, waiting outside a lingerie shop for his wife and holding their baby – or, more specifically, holding the pushchair – when an altercation at a nearby muffin stall distracted him. As he restored order to the tipped-over kiosk, a recently bereaved mother plucked the child and walked off into the deep cavern of the centre. Exiting the shop, his wife was confronted with the following scene: her husband, a raspberry muffin in his hand, horror on his face, and only a twisted white blanket where the baby had once been.

'Not funny,' he said to Larry. 'You'll be sorry you said that.'

2.

I was seventeen and in mourning for a first love gone awry.

Jessica and I had only gone out for three months, but it's wrong to measure first relationships in units of time. So I'll put it this way: when we broke up, it felt like I lost thirty pints of blood. Am I being over the top? Yes. But in the aftermath, I genuinely felt drained and unwell. I

watched *Man on the Moon* six times in three days and
– in a severe bout of confusion – I believed I was the
American comedian Andy Kaufman. (Rationally, I knew
I wasn't him, but part of me suspected I was. It was a
strange doublethink, like being six years old and recog-
nising my sister's handwriting in Father Christmas's letters, and yet still believing.) Anyway, after the break-up
with Jessica, I had – in my Kaufman-confusion – arranged
a town wrestling contest where I fought women and
only women. On a big patch of grass beside Caerphilly
Castle I assembled a makeshift wrestling ring, and each
Saturday would charge £1.50 for a female to wrestle me.
I pasted posters to the windows of long-closed-down
shops, and advertised in large lettering the prize: £50
and an offer to organise the winner's personal finances.
(I was very good at maths.)

And I also happened to be pretty good at the wrestling. I made £27 on my first day of bouts, and a further
£75 in the weeks after. But it all came to an end one
shiny-wet May evening when a large woman fell on my
collarbone, and snapped it in two.

I spent the next month and a half in a sling.

3.

I should explain what preceded the attempted arrest.

Gareth had wanted to leave town for the weekend.
His cousin Robert had just died from blood poisoning,

and he – Gareth – had, in a dark alley beside the chip shop, taken the virginity of a fifteen-year-old girl and was convinced he now had Aids. He booked an STI test, but it was going to take four weeks before the clinic would put the cocktail umbrella down his penis.

He had called with the plan. We were to meet outside his aunt's home (he was living there after falling out with his father again) and then walk to the hills to camp for the evening.

Lacking an air bed, Larry decided to bring a dinghy.

'*A sleep fit for a fish*,' he said to me in a text message.

Gareth and I were content to sleep out on the ground. It was a hot summer – they always were then – and I'd read and seen countless stories and films where kids slept outside under starlit skies.

But when I arrived at the aunt's home, I found Larry crouched down behind a Jeep, with the dinghy and oar on the pavement. He put his finger to his lips and sig-nalled with his other hand to join him. I thought he was only messing, and I walked towards the front door. He grabbed me by the shirt and pulled me back behind the car.

'The neighbour's gone mad,' he whispered. 'He's kicked the door in.'

'The neighbour?' I said.

'Yeah, he's a nutcase.'

He pointed towards the aunt's house, to the broken glass on the patio – scattered like breadcrumbs left out for the birds – and before it, the dark hulking shape of a man gone mad.

4.

A few weeks before all this, when I started crying in a maths lesson because of stories involving Jessica and a local bus driver, Larry had put an arm around me and said, 'A good wank is what you need. A good wank and some tits in your face.'

He took me to a St Martin's sixth-form party at the rugby club, and because we were all so intimidated by the beauty of alien flesh, Larry insisted we play Pull the Bull.

'Tenner for whoever gets the ugliest,' he said.

'But how will we decide?' I asked, picturing the first time I watched Jessica put her clothes back on in the morning, her pale legs mapped with little white scores. 'Is beauty or its opposite not a subjective thing?'

'Public vote,' he said.

We lined up on one side of the dance floor, like men in BBC-Jane-Austen-adaptation-dances, and looked for misshapen faces, buck teeth, and poorly applied mascara.

Gareth was the first to thrust himself into the evening. He kissed a girl who – in Larry's words – was 'a five out of ten'. And as he got with the girl, Gareth gave us the finger behind her back, cockily convinced the £10 prize was coming his way. I approached a pale girl with dark hair who reminded me of Jessica, but when she asked

THOMAS MORRIS

me my name I couldn't speak – the sounds got stuck between my tongue and teeth.

Then Larry, driven by his usual dickishness, sashayed onto the dance floor with a short, stubby girl. The ensuing commotion confused me, but when she turned around it all made sense. She was one of the St Martin's girls' older sisters. She had Down's syndrome, and Larry and her were dancing – hand in hand, hips touching, his crotch rubbing against her leg. I watched him move his face closer and closer to her face, move his hand to her cheek, and stroke the rose hairclip at the side of her head. With a finger, he brushed her blonde fringe from her eyes. Then he dipped his mouth, and within seconds they were kissing.

After we'd been kicked out, and Larry collected the money off us, he pleaded his case.

'I don't discriminate,' he said. 'Plus she was one of those that go to college and study how to look after themselves. She can catch buses and everything.'

We walked into the cold dark night, my recently healed collarbone aching, and Gareth arguing that his girl was still uglier. I was thinking too much about Jessica to realise there was anything wrong with what we'd done.

5.

From behind the Jeep, Larry and I watched the neighbour climb back over the wall and calmly disappear into his own house like a button passing through a hole.

When I knocked, I heard Gareth stop dead in the hall. I shouted through the front door – literally *through* the door: half the glass had shattered – that it was me, to let me and Larry in.

'He went mad,' Gareth whispered, as we sat in conference in the living room. 'I was playing music, nothing too loud, and then—'

'The door went smash,' said Larry, standing up. 'His foot his head his shoulder. The door went smash.'

'He used to be a copper,' said Gareth. 'But he got thrown off the force for using *too much* force.'

'Fuck,' I said. 'Really?'

'We should get the hell out,' Gareth murmured. 'Before he comes back to finish me off.'

'Do you reckon he will?' I said.

'I dunno,' Gareth said, removing his glasses and rubbing his eyes. 'His wife left him a week ago and he's been a fucking psycho ever since. He stays up till six in the morning listening to country-and-western songs. I can hear him singing "Blue Moon" through my bedroom wall.'

Larry swiped the air with the oar.

'If he comes back, I'll bash him,' he said. And we all laughed, giddy with the fear.

'My aunt's going to go nuts about the front door, though,' said Gareth. 'She warned me to keep the noise down cos of him. Seriously, she's gonna kill me. Well, if the Aids don't get me first.'

'For fuck's sake,' said Larry. 'You don't have Aids.'

'I do,' Gareth said quietly. 'I can feel it in my dick.'

He didn't want to leave our stuff in the house, so we settled on taking the bags, the dinghy, and the oar, and running to the nearest phone box or friendly stranger.

'Fine,' I said. 'But I need a piss first.'

In the bathroom, above the toilet, I saw a photo of Gareth as a child, his arm resting ever so slightly round the neck of his now-dead cousin. I looked down at my penis and felt sad for its loneliness.

When I returned to the living room, Gareth had his boxer shorts over his jeans.

'My idea,' explained Larry, doing up his coat. 'It's a confusion tactic. If the guy is out there, he'll be stunned by the boxers. And in that split second of confusion – BAM! – oar to the head.'

We laughed again, geed each other up, and after many aborted beginnings, finally ran out the front door.

That's when we heard the sirens and thought we were saved.

6.

The things I cannot shake: the walk to the bus depot; the erections so stiff I feared the foreskin would never unroll; the fingering of vomit in a circular motion down a sink. The antibacterial soap Jessica carried in her bag; and the way she cleaned her hands after every meal, every cigarette. The toothbrush she left in my bathroom and the deodorant, which I started using, sniffing myself in maths lessons. The fifteen-page letter I wrote, and the four-line reply. The anger on the women's faces as they lay in the shadow of the castle, pinned to the ground by a seventeen-year-old boy.

7.

'Why won't you tell us your name?' the bald policeman asked through the half-opened window. 'What are you hiding?'

'I have a – uh – uh – sssstammer,' I answered, then took a breath as deep as a bucket. 'Nay-nay-names are the most di-di-di-difficult things for a stammerer to say.'

'Is that so?'

'I can write it duh-duh-duh-duh.' My voice was like a locked gate, so I took a singing breath and bounced the words off one other: 'I-can-write-it-down-for-you-though,' I said.

'Get the cocky one over here,' the bald cop called to the Elvis quiff. And quicker than a mistake, Larry was sitting beside me in the back of the car.

'He can't talk tidy,' Larry said. 'He's a bit thick.'

'I'm not thick.'

The smirk of the bald. The pulse of the vein in his temple.

'And his name?'

'Reg Harrison, sir.'

'Reg? A fifteen-year-old named Reg?'

'I'm seventeen,' I said. 'And my nuh-name isn't Reg.'

Baldilocks shook his head and walked off.

'Gareth's shitting it,' said Larry.

'Aren't you?' My stammer was like a well-trained dog: it knew who to bark at.

Larry laughed. 'He reckons they're gonna search the bags. He just told me he's got the T-shirt from last week in there. The one covered in blood.'

'Blood?'

'You know, the one he was wearing when he shagged that girl. He wanted to burn it up the mountain tonight. Doesn't the one with the quiff look like Elvis?'

'Fuck,' I said.

'Yeah,' he said. 'He's scared they'll trace the blood and arrest him for being a paedo.'

'Shh,' I said. 'What if they're recording everything we say?'

'Screw them,' he said. 'We've done shit-all wrong.'

And that's when Larry found the police hat in the back of the car. The proper helmet kind. The ones kids wear when they're dressing up.

'Dare me to put it on,' he said, poking me with one long finger.

'No.'

'Aw, go on. I bet Elvis would love to see me in his hat.'

'Fuck off,' I said.

He leaned over the seat and slipped it on, then looked at himself in the rear-view mirror. He curled his lip, and out the side of it he sang: '*Aha-ha*, I'm all shook up.'

8.

I'd known it was love when Jessica confessed that she wanted to have a black friend. I too had known this feeling, had wanted to prove myself in our small, white town.

We were at a house party, and when she asked my name I answered liked I had never stammered in my life.

We left the party early, broke into a park, and lay on the grass, dry-humping for at least an hour. She allowed me to touch her breasts and she felt me through my jeans. She tasted of smoke and spearmint, and by the end of the humping my dick was sore from all the chafing. But when she washed the mud off her hands with her mini bottle of soap, I felt the gush of new blood that comes with first love. We kissed a little more, and then I walked her to the bus station, the streetlamps glowing like electric lunchboxes. The next day we started going out.

It's not my place to go into the stuff she had going on, but it's enough to say she was depressed. I couldn't see it at the time, not because I was shallow or didn't care – I wasn't, and I did – but a lot of my friends were cutting themselves, even Gareth, so it didn't seem like a big deal. Of course, it seems stupid to say that now, but I think it was important to her that it didn't bother me.

In a way, I think that's why she liked me.

But because of her depression, at the beginning, she was the one in control. She'd also had sex before, and knew about bands and films and real sadness, and next to her I sometimes felt like a catalogue model – clean-cut, without history.

And she was a hundred times more gifted than me. She played the harp, and I'd watch and listen to her play in the living room for hours at a time, her fingers doing all sorts of mad things on the strings. Other days, we'd spend whole afternoons in her bedroom as she smoked dope and told stories about lucid dreaming, ex-boyfriends, and the time she got so stoned she couldn't talk for a day. In the evenings, we'd sneak into Caerphilly Castle and go up one of the tall towers to smoke weed. A few weeks in, she made me climb over a barrier and stand on the ledge of the tower. She climbed over, too.

'If you held me from behind it'd be like that scene in *Titanic*,' she said. 'But a bit less shit.'

We could see all of Caerphilly: the shopping centre, Tesco, and the mountains all around. The Welsh flag flapped wildly in the wind, and I felt outside and above myself, like I was watching us in some made-for-schools film about the dangers of drugs. But when the wind got stronger and I wanted to get off the ledge, she insisted we stay. We looked down at the moat – it was as black as her hair – and she pointed at an upturned shopping trolley, jutting out in the shallows.

'Looks like a ribcage, doesn't it?' she said, lighting a joint. 'God, imagine being that thin.'

'As thin as a shopping trolley?' I said.

'You know what I mean,' she said, and went to pass the joint, but I shook my head.

She looked at me, smiled, pretended to fall, then actually slipped. I caught her, but the lighter dropped into the moat with a plop.

'Oh my,' she said.

I looked at her face, and then she intoned in a funny deep voice:

> *'Do not go gentle into that good night,*
> *rage, rage against the dying of the lighter.'*

On an afternoon when we both should have been in school, she finally took my virginity. In my childhood bed, with the peeling, faded stickers of Mr Men and Teenage Mutant Ninja Turtles on the headboard, she guided me, showed me what to do. At one stage I could have sworn that Michelangelo, pizza in hand, gave me a little wink.

Afterwards, as she dressed, and her scarred arms vanished into long black sleeves, she smiled and said thanks.

'Thanks for what?' I said.

'Thanks for not being a dick.'

9.

Oh, how those women tumbled on the grass in front of the castle!

10.

The Quiff was in the driver's seat, and Larry and I were in the back, silent. Every now and then a woman's voice came over the police radio, and the Quiff would nod his head knowingly. Gareth was still outside, sitting against the garden wall, as the bald one strolled to and fro on the pavement, asking questions and writing things in a notebook.

'How long have you all known each other, then?' said the Quiff. He was staring at the mad neighbour's house.

'Since nuh-nuh-nursery,' I said. 'And then we all went to the same primary school and now-now-now we're all at the same secondary school too.'

His hat lay at Larry's feet.

'That's nice,' said the Quiff, still looking out the windscreen, as if the street and houses were a TV show. 'Yeah, it's good to have old friends.'

The detective arrived in an unmarked car, and the Quiff got out to talk to him. The detective was tall and thin and had a big nose. He shone a flashlight beneath the Jeep, and the beam fell upon the oar – discarded by

Larry when the sirens first sounded. With a tentative scooping of an outstretched leg, the Quiff pulled back the oar.

'Bingo bango,' said the bald one. 'We have a weapon.'

'Great stuff,' said the detective. 'Case closed.' He got back into his car and left.

I felt a clutch at my ribs, a sagging of my lungs.

Outside my window, the moon was full as an egg.

11.

We saw each other every day and I became part of Jessica's family. On weekends she played the harp at weddings, and I'd sit in the back pews feeling a mixture of pride and distance, as if her talent would always keep us separate from one another. After each performance, she'd buy a bag of weed with the money she'd earned, and apply superglue to her cracked and bleeding fingers. The first time I touched her glued fingertips, they felt unreal. ('No prints,' she said, moving her fingers in the air. 'I'd make the perfect thief.')

She grew more comfortable with me, and in turn became more confident. She started wearing short-sleeved tops, and didn't even care when Larry asked her what had happened to her arms.

But once my virginity was gone I grew hungry with the loss, and I'd try to turn every innocent kiss into the start of foreplay. And as she became more confident in her body, I (believing myself to be responsible for her transformation) became cocky. And when that happened, the balance between us shifted: as I became the confident one, she became clingy. And I grew attached to being needed and I abused the feeling. On evenings when she was really down, I feigned illness, fatigue, anything that would elicit her desperation. I would leave her house early, to have her beg me to stay.

I started speaking with girls in chat rooms, on webcams, anywhere I could. I thought of doing things to these other girls, of exotic positions, of so many different breasts. I had had sex with one person and now I was ready to have sex with the world. And though I was in love, I mourned the fact I wasn't single. So I boasted to Gareth and Larry about oral sex and the frequency with which I received it. I knew it was ungracious but it bubbled up inside me like bile.

12.

It took a while to understand what the police suspected.

'Attempted burglary,' the bald one said at last. 'You could go down for eight years for this.'

I pictured the courtroom, the cell, the release at twenty-five with a wizened face that wasn't my own.

My eyeballs sat heavy in their sockets.

Gareth had left the key in the house, and they wouldn't let us ring anyone, so we couldn't prove the house belonged to his aunt. In the oar they thought they'd found a weapon for smashing the door, and the dinghy, what? – a possible means of escape? Were we going to row our way to freedom?

The neighbours across the road were the ones who had heard the shouting and the smashing. They'd looked from behind their velvet curtains and seen a figure kicking the door. They had called the police, but now weren't sure if there'd been one person or more.

Oh, we were being had, alright.

13.

I was drunk deep to my stomach and wearing vomit on my sleeve, when I made the biggest mistake. We were at a silver-surfaced club, where songs by Usher seemed to be on loop. Jessica had lost her phone, an expensive birthday present from her father, and she was in tears. I meant to say to her that it was okay, that we'd find it, but all that came out of my staggering mouth was: 'I love you.'

'Oh, you'll be better in the morning,' she said, patting my head. 'Now, come on, let's find my phone.'

That evening, at her father's house and with Jessica still phoneless, we had unprotected sex and twice fell off the bed. I tried taking her from behind but didn't know what I was doing. I moved her limbs every which way. But still confused by it all, I grew frustrated and complained about the lack of moisture.

In the morning, awakening to an empty house and emboldened by the intimacy of the night before, I left the bathroom door open while I peed. Passing in the hall, she rested a hand on the newel post, looked at me and sighed.

I don't know if it was the love or the sex, but after that night we saw less of each other. At a house party a week later she got so drunk and so stoned that she passed out on the living-room floor and threw up all over herself. With Larry's help, I carried her to the bathroom. I sat her up, her head over the toilet bowl, and from her hair I picked out bits of vomited pasta. All the while she was somehow still asleep. In the morning I asked her how she felt.

'Pretty good,' she said, 'but who the hell threw up on my clothes?'

I lectured her. I made a martyr out of myself. I wrote a poem about it and sent it to her in an email.

'I'm not sure I like the tone of this poem,' she replied. 'But I like the way you rhymed "pasta-remnants conditioned hair" with "do you ever care?" – that was nice.'

She grew distant. She started spending time with older people. And the tendon in my ear and the jut of my jaw both ached from the phone calls I kept making to her home.

And when she broke up with me, the feeling that peeked out – like a hilltop above it all – was guilt for wanting to sleep with other girls during our time together. It was like when I was seven and spent a week in a Welsh-language heritage camp. There were sheep living in the garden, and I silently wished I had a sheep – instead of my blind and stupid dog – only to return home a few days later to find that Rosie had died, had been cremated on Bonfire Night by my father.

14.

A few days after the Pull the Bull party, Larry ran into the girl with Down's syndrome at the shopping centre. He told us she hugged him, put her arms around him and kissed his cheek.

Her mother apologised and pulled the girl away. But Larry assured her that it was okay, that it happened to him all the time – he said he must have one of those faces. The mother smiled and – I really doubted this part – gave Larry a scone from a clear bag of cakes.

He said he ate half and fed the rest to the ducks in the castle moat.

I don't know why, but this scene has always stayed with me.

15.

They wouldn't believe us.

'It was the guy next door,' Gareth said.

'We've asked him,' the bald one answered. 'He told us he only just got in.'

'Bullshit.'

'Watch your language,' Elvis said. 'And that's a serious allegation you're making against Former Constable Spencer there. Think carefully before you repeat it. Now, one more time, what were you doing on the property?'

Gareth told them to look in the house, to see the photos of him on the mantelpiece, but they just ignored his pleas. They finally permitted him to call his aunt, but she didn't answer. She was still at her meeting with the bereavement group. We could hear everything – or almost everything – from the back of the car.

Larry, meanwhile, had the policeman's hat back on and was admiring himself in the mirror.

'Allo, allo, allo,' he said, stroking the hat.

'Do you ever take anything seriously?' I said.

He turned to me slowly. 'No,' he said, 'never.'

'Gareth should just call his parents,' I said. 'They could sort all this out.'

'Nah, his old man's as crazy as the neighbour,' he said. 'God, as if they were ever going to arrest a former cop. It's ridiculous.'

'I just don't get why they're keeping us here,' I said. 'Unless—'

'Unless what?'

'Do you reckon they know about you kissing the Down's syndrome girl?'

He carried on watching himself in the mirror, stroking his tufts of hair.

'Nope,' he said. 'Anyway, not even illegal.'

'What about the fifteen-year-old in the alley?' I said.

'Doubt it.' He leaned over the seat and fiddled with the radio. 'Do you reckon we can get Radio 1 on this?'

He found a clear frequency – a woman's voice talking about a disturbance at the castle.

'Eight years in prison?' he said, sitting back and adjusting the hat. 'I could do that in my sleep.'

Outside, the police were laughing.

16.

After I broke my collarbone, and word of my wrestling had spread, I was called in to see the headmaster.

'Is everything alright?' he asked. On the wall behind him was a poster of a wolf, a sheep, a bag of a grain, two islands and a boat, and the words: 'There's Always a Solution'. The sling chafed my neck and my armpit smelled.

'Absolutely perfect,' I said. 'Couldn't be better.'

'I'm just concerned,' the headmaster said. 'We've had reports of you trying to arm-wrestle the dinner ladies.'

'Those were private words shared in private.'

'I see,' he said. 'Do you know what you'll do when you're finished with school?'

'I will become a useful contributor to society.'

'And the wrestling?'

'That too may still have a role,' I said. 'It's a bit early to tell.'

'Anything else you want to tell me?'

'As a matter of fact, yes,' I said. 'I'm tired of waking up at 7 a.m. And I'm tired of making breakfast, eating breakfast, getting dressed, brushing my teeth, walking to the bus, getting on the bus, giving money to the driver, sitting on the bus, coming to school, going to lessons and staying there as the day grows darker. My legs are tired and my hips are tired, and my ankles are aching, and my head always feels like I've just done an exam. I find it hard to keep focused on a thought without thinking about thinking about that thought. And I'm finding it hard even talking to you now. And you know what I'm most tired of? Knowing that this is just the start, that I'll only get more tired as I get older, that I'll have a life of being—'

There was no school counsellor so I wasn't referred to one.

I was glad of that.

17.

And though I wouldn't find out about Jessica until the morning after, I remember exactly those seventeen words that came over the police radio:

'Quit messing those kids and come to the castle,' the voice said. 'We've found a body in the fucking moat.'

CLAP HANDS

Because the state will always find new ways to make no sense, Amy couldn't work more than eighteen hours a week. Well, she could have, but because of the child tax credits, each hour she worked beyond the eighteen hours was taken back off her in tax. So mornings at the nursery were fine. The rest of her life was a full-time job anyway: her husband had just run off and left her with their three kids; the house was falling apart; her mother was still percolating after her father's death; and having heroically, majestically, failed the test five times in four years, she still couldn't drive.

It might sound like we're piling it on, but this is how life lived in Amy: with spider legs, scuttling in all directions.

*

The nursery was in the community hall beside the castle. Stacks of chairs and foldaway tables edged the room, and the kids had to be constantly stopped from climbing all over them. There was a stage at the back of the hall, and that too was a temptation. At least once a day some child would scale the five steps up to the stage, ready to jump off – only to be lifted down at the last minute by Amy or Pam or Nicole.

Amy'd arrive at 9 a.m to set up. From the damp shed beside the hall, she and Pam and Nicole would extract the bikes, the doll houses, and all the rest of the toys, and lay them out in the hall. Though every so often the shed would get broken into and the kids had to suffer weeks with miserable toys until the insurance people paid out.

Half nine was when the children arrived, swaddled in their coats and scarves. As the first children turned up, Nicole – at the nursery on a training scheme – would head to the small kitchen and make coffee. She hadn't been instructed to do this, but she understood that coffee was what was needed.

The kids loved Nicole. They would hug her legs, hold her hand, ask her to be their mum. She was twenty-one and had spent so long in the care system that a whole wing of Caerphilly social services should have been named after her. But she always acted positive, like a change of wind was just around the corner. If you had read her case notes you'd have thought she was stupid *not* to think that buckets of tragedy were perched on every half-opened door she approached. She could sing, though, and dance and draw. ('If they had offered GCSEs in that stuff I woulda been the best in the school,' she said often in various ways.)

Pam, meanwhile, was on hand to settle disputes – mainly between the two boys who always argued over the big bike. Before joining the nursery, Pam had worked in the tax office for ten years. She said there was very little difference between the two jobs.

Amy was the nursery leader, and she usually tried to keep at a small distance, so as to be able to watch over things. But more often than not she spent her mornings on her hunkers, attempting to coax a word from the mournfully shy girl who wouldn't talk to anyone. And, all the while, the boy who liked to play with dolls would pull at Amy's jumper, insisting that she help him organise the 'tea party'. There were twenty-four children at the nursery, and to the untrained eye the community hall was a wild chaos. But Amy often imagined that if she viewed it all from above, she'd see grand and elegant designs in the paths the children tore.

At food-and-drink time, Pam took charge. She complained about the spilled milk, about the ground-in bourbons and custard creams, and the parents who didn't teach their kids to eat properly. But Amy always spied a little smile on Pam's face as she baby-wiped a child's fingers and asked them if they'd enjoyed their biscuit. After food, Amy would then lead the directed learning: phonics and numbers and guided playing with bricks and puzzles, while Pam and Nicole took the kids in turns to the freezer-cold toilets where the taps dripped ice water. If it were a special occasion, like Christmas or

Mother's Day, they'd spend an hour with the kids making cards, gluing and glittering and crayoning until the tables and the children were sticky and sparkling.

And each day ended on the carpet, as Amy (and increasingly Nicole) led song-time and goodbyes (while Pam quietly put the place back in order). Then, at 12.30, parents and grandparents returned to pick up their left-luggage kids.

Same again next day, with explanations to a different parent about a head hit on a table corner or banged against the stage. And same again the next day: rinse, dry, repeat, etc.

*

For Amy, afternoons were filled with more acute challenges – like dealing with her mother, or driving lessons, or trying not to have a panic attack as she stood in front of the ATM, in that pause between hitting ENTER and waiting for the chugging of cash drawers to start, a chugging that sometimes felt like it would never begin. One time, when there had been nothing in the account but the solitary beeping of Insufficient Funds, and Amy was panic-reeling, a random man said to her – like it was his own idea, his very own words – 'Cheer up, it might never happen.'

She studied him – his smug eyes and his smug hair and his smug little smile.

'Well, you're *wrong*,' she said. 'It *has* happened.'

The man stuttered apologies and darted down the road.

So yes, some afternoons were spent taking her shrinking mother to Safeway (having no car meant doing the weekly shop in stages and bits) and other afternoons consisted of accompanying her on the bus to the doctor's or the hospital or the solicitor's, or doing endless rounds of washing. Other days were taken up entirely with calls and meetings with the CSA and the DSS and the Citizen's Advice Bureau and the tax office and Swalec and BT and British Gas and Abbey National – and then doing all this and more for her mother, too. Amy seemed to spend most of her time sitting on the bottom stair in the hall, the phone resting between her chin and shoulder as she scrawled down the names and numbers of people and departments to call. The twirling of the phone's curly wire around her fingers – and even the smell of the hall itself – slowly became synonymous with disappointment: it only ever connected her and the house to more problems.

And problems, she learned, did not need an invite.

*

In the evenings, after fixing food for her kids – Rhys (8), Will (12) and Gemma (14) – she'd often fall asleep for an hour or so on the living-room couch, waking up to the sound of a tennis-ball thud against the side wall. Rhys was convinced he was going to make it profession-al, and he withdrew books from the library – old yellow books with crouching men in old-fashioned shorts hold-ing wooden rackets on the covers – to hone his skills. And at night, as Gemma and Will did their homework, or half-killed each other over who got to use the com-puter, Rhys played tennis against the outside wall.

The guy at the tennis club told Amy that Rhys need-ed one-on-one training sessions that cost £16 an hour, maybe two or three times a week, to stand any chance of making it. But the £4 Friday group sessions were enough of a stretch money-wise. Amy began to wonder if it was cruel to encourage him when she knew how it would all end. But she'd made a vow to bite her tongue, to not become her mother. And Rhys was still young. It didn't seem right to submerge him in the language and logic of lifelong letdowns.

Anyway, he'd learn soon enough.

*

What else haven't we mentioned? Of course, Peter. Yes, he described it as feeling like a cascade of broken glass. He said he felt like he was going mad, like he didn't know who or what he was any more. He had grown up in a family without love, and he didn't know how to feel it, or how to give it. He had to find himself, he said. And he had an inkling that the real him might be hiding in Australia. Hence the leaving, hence the no child-maintenance, hence the remortgaging a few months before departing – and Amy's new unofficial title as sole mortgage owner. But he said he would do right by the kids. He would send money back as soon as money came his way. Six months whipped and trundled, and he did indeed send money – £78, then, three months later, £20 for Gemma's birthday.

Oh, livid wasn't the word.

And among these spindly spider legs, the electric kept going off. A trip switch blowing, or dropping, or whatever it is they do. Amy wedged a broomstick on a step-ladder up against it, but no joy. The switch kept blowing out, then breathing in, extinguishing lights and resetting alarm clocks to 00:00.

*

And time did seem to move oddly during all this. The days would disappear but the nights would be heavy and slow, and the weeks would drag but the months would bunch up, spilling over each other like they were all racing for the new year. Then, one frosty morning, as she was taking the toys out of the shed, Nicole announced she was trying to trace her mother.

'I know it's stupid,' she said, carrying out the toy oven. 'I could turn up at her door and she could just tell me to piss off, but, like, once you find out somethin' like this, you've gotta do somethin', haven't you?'

Pam took the oven off her and rested it on the ground. 'I dunno if you should get into all that,' she said. 'You hear some right horror stories about people meeting their real parents.'

Amy watched Nicole's eyes as she tried to keep it together. 'God, I dunno,' Nicole said. 'Am I being a stupid tit?'

Amy waited till later, until she got Nicole on her own. 'You should do it,' she told her. 'But see how things go, and take it slow. You're the one you've got to protect.'

*

And while Gemma began writing environmental poetry, and Will began obscuring half his face with a fringe, Rhys started entering proper tennis tournaments. On the mornings of the competitions, he'd cover his cornflakes with sugar for extra energy, then sit in the kitchen, listening to Tina Turner on Gemma's Discman.

At a tournament in Ystrad Mynach he reached the quarter-finals and played a boy with rosy cheeks and quaffed hair, who Will reckoned looked like a 'miniature lawyer'. Amy suspected there must have been an odd hippy strain in the boy's family because his T-shirt design was a map of the world – all greens and blues. She generally couldn't watch the matches. She'd get too nervous. But Gemma insisted that she watch this one. As Rhys and the lawyer-boy warmed-up – hitting balls back and forth – Amy began to see the match as if it were a class war, or some divine precursor of her family's fate.

Rhys went ahead, and then he went behind, and then he went ahead again. At one stage he looked over at them all and winked. Whilst preparing to serve, he'd point his foot to the furthest net-post, and then bounce the ball three or four times before the toss. Amy thought he looked composed, way more composed than she ever felt herself.

It was a close match. Rhys would hit a few brilliant shots and then the other boy would retaliate with a strong backhand or some odd, sliced forehand. Amy hadn't seen Rhys play in a while, but he had improved so much. He looked confident, easy.

He was up a break, and close to finishing out the match when he missed an easy enough volley. Then he double faulted, and started talking to himself and pacing back and forth. At the change of ends he went to his rucksack and took out one of the good red towels from home. Amy watched him wipe his racket, his face, and each finger individually.

The match went to a tiebreak. And it was really tight again – both of them breaking each other's serve – until Rhys fell over at 4–4. And that was it. He lost his head, he was gone.

The lawyer-boy went to the net and proffered his hand. But Rhys wouldn't take it. He started arguing with the umpire. Amy came over to calm him down, but he was raging. He demanded to talk to the tournament organisers. He said that the other boy had broken the rules, that he should have been wearing all white, that it was impossible to pick out the ball against his blue and green T-shirt. And Amy, too, found herself oddly incensed. She was marching up to the clubhouse, with Rhys, Gemma and Will bustling beside her, when she finally caught hold of herself.

'Oh, let's just go home,' she said. 'Come on, we'll get milkshakes as a treat.'

On the bus back, Rhys cried for twenty minutes straight. Amy could feel the headache ramming inside his little-boy skull.

'His mum made him wear the T-shirt,' he said, as he sucked on his straw. They were in the Wimpy on Cardiff Road, the black night falling over the traffic and the shops.

'What do you mean?' said Will.

'He wore it on purpose,' Rhys said. 'It was all part of their plan.'

The following Monday, Rhys pushed his hand through the glass of his bedroom window, angry at being made to go to bed when Liverpool were playing. A few days later, he threw a mirror out the bathroom window for reasons Amy never quite unearthed; and finally, ultimately, when *Neighbours* was on one evening, he came downstairs with a tennis racket and smashed in the screen.

'Fuck *Neighbours*,' he said. 'Fuck Australia.'

She pushed him into more sports, into football and rugby and athletics. She'd walk him down to the sports centre two or three times a week, and wait in the cafe, sipping the same coffee for an hour, watching groups of health-blushed mothers with yoga mats and tote bags.

She'd think: they look stupid.

She'd think: I actually wouldn't mind trying yoga.

Ah, she'd think: school trips, heating bills, driving lessons.

Well, maybe she could learn to do yoga at home.

*

And then, one rainy evening, as Amy was staring at a dark stain on the ceiling, Rhys called down from the bath. When she reached the landing, the door crept open, her son's quizzical head popped around, and his breaking voice said:

'There's mushrooms growing by the toilet.'

And indeed, mushrooms they were! Some kind of fungi spurting out beside the basin of the loo, between the floorboards and the wall. When Amy called the council, they sent a short man with a thick moustache. He brought his own son along, a little boy, seven or eight, wearing glasses and a mini plumber's outfit – blue overalls, the works. The man put on a pair of see-through gloves, stroked the mushrooms and sighed.

'Ah yes,' he said. 'That's global warming, that is.'

'What the hell you on about?' she said, and the little boy looked up to his dad, as if he wondered the same.

'Bathrooms get very humid,' he said. 'Because the world's heating up, you see.'

'You being serious?' she said.

The man looked at the floor, his brows furrowed. 'Aww God, mun,' he sighed. 'I can't do this.' He took off his gloves and lay them on the toolbox.

'Can't do what?' she said.

He sat down on the floor then, with his back against the wall. He scratched his face and rubbed his moustache. He looked as if he was about to cry.

'I'll be honest with you, love,' he said. 'Me and the boy, we don't know what we're doing.'

'You what?' she said.

'We're not plumbers,' he said. 'I'm pretty good round the house, so for some extra money I thought I'd give it a go. But it's quite clear I'm already out of my depth.'

She rubbed her eyes, took a deep breath, and brought the father and his son downstairs to the living room. She gave the man a cup of tea, and the boy a glass of squash. She made them a ham sandwich each, and sat on the couch as they ate at the table. Neither said a word, and the two stared off into the distance as they chewed, nodding their heads slowly, like they were both thinking their saddest thoughts, the thoughts they'd enter if they had to cry.

'Well, we'd better be going,' the man said eventually. 'Thanks for the tea.'

'Yeah,' added the boy. 'Thanks for the sandwich, too.'

When the council sent a real plumber, he saw the problem for what it was – a leaking pipe, a rotting joist, a bloody big mess. And so began the grant-application process, which led to seven weeks of more phone calls and letters, of appointments and visits, of a building site for a home, and daily family trips to Gran's house for baths and showers.

*

At the height of the plumbing and building work, Nicole came into the nursery with a letter. They had found her mother. Amy wasn't quite sure who 'they' were.

'Does she want to see you?' she said. 'Does she know you're looking for her?'

'She's living in Abertridwr,' Nicole said. 'All this time, and she's been two miles up the road. I'm gonna call her tonight.'

Pam was from Abertridwr. She asked to see the letter.

'Katrina Jones,' Pam said, her eyes scanning the page. 'How do I know that name?'

Throughout the day, Amy tried to manage Nicole's

expectations. For all her cockiness, Nicole was fragile. She'd had five sets of foster parents growing up, had been in care twice, and – though she was always unclear about it – Amy and Pam were sure she'd been abused.

After food, when they were sat at the table making Easter cards with the kids, Amy told Nicole to just think it through.

'Seriously,' she said, 'mothers are hard work at the best of times.'

'Ah, I'll be fine,' Nicole said, dabbing glue onto yellow cotton wool. 'Anyway, if she starts trying to kill me, I'll ring you straight away.'

So Nicole went ahead and met her mother. And each day she came in with a different story, recounting the hilarious things said and done the night before. Within a few weeks, Katrina had moved in with her. It was going well; in fact, Nicole said, they were *getting on like a burning house*.

*

Around this time, Castle Cabs changed their number. Now it was just a single digit different to Amy's, and the house phone rang at all hours: people looking to get home, or to get out, or just be in a different place to where they were.

Amy'd apologise and tell the callers they had the wrong

number. On a few occasions, people asked her to come and collect them anyway. Sometimes Will would urge her to go and pick them up. And if she could have driven, Amy genuinely would have done it. She'd have done most things for some extra money. But she had never been good with cars. And only recently she'd had a nightmare in which she was driving a giant lorry through Caerphilly, but she was sat at the back of the truck, and she couldn't see the road, and instead of a steering wheel she had a PlayStation control pad and she had to guess what the traffic was like.

'I'm sorry,' she repeatedly told the stranded taxi-wanters. To one woman, she found herself saying: 'If I could I would, but I can't.'

*

The Friday before May half-term, Nicole brought Katrina into the nursery. Katrina had scraped-back short hair, and looked like she'd seen some things. Things that were unlikely to appear in the *Radio Times*. She spoke with a husk. And her skin was conkerish in colour, and tight, taut, the same quality of face Amy's father had when he was still alive. It was unmistakable, really. And meeting Katrina brought all those things back to Amy. The sadnesses and the embarrassments, but also the serrated laughs, the points of hysteria where there's nothing left but laughs: like the time when she was sixteen and found her father topless, flat-out on the landing, a ready-meal beside him on a plate. He was surely dead. But then he slowly stirred and urged Amy to 'go fetch a glass of council pop'.

But Katrina was good with the kids. She was wild, yes: she swung one of boys around a hundred miles a hour, and Amy honestly thought his arms were going to fling out of their sockets. But the boy loved it, and an orderly queue promptly formed behind him – an unfurled necklace of children wanting a thrill they couldn't get at home.

And while all the children mobbed Katrina, Pam took Amy aside.

'It just came to me now,' she said, in a quiet voice. 'I remember how I know the name. Katrina was a few years below me in school. She used to give out handjobs for a pound.'

Amy watched Katrina throw a boy in the air and catch him.

'She used to go down town at lunchtime,' Pam said. 'That was bad enough, cos only sixth-formers were allowed, and Katrina was only fourteen. But then she'd do whatever with some guy in the back of his van, and go buy her dinner with the money. You'd see her sometimes, walking back up the hill, eating a bag of chips.'

When it was milk-and-biscuits time Katrina came up to Amy, took her hand and held it tight.

'I just wanted to say thank you,' she said. 'I know you and Pam have been so good to her.'

They were both watching Nicole. She was teaching three little girls to belly dance, her hands at her head, her body gyrating.

'No, no,' Amy said. 'She's a great girl.'

'I named her Amy, you know,' Katrina said. 'When she was born, I mean.'

Amy didn't know what to say.

'He wanted nothing to do with us, you see,' Katrina said. 'And none of my family did either. I was totally broke, I had nothing.'

'You don't have to—'

'Honestly, love. There was nothing I could do. I thought about her all the time, but I was waiting, you know? Until I felt ready. I didn't want to ruin her life all over again.'

Before Amy could say anything, a boy whizzed past and Katrina picked him up and spun him around in circles.

At noon, they sat the kids down at the carpet for songs and goodbyes. They sang the usuals: nursery rhymes and the like, but then Katrina took the quiet girl onto her lap and sang, over and over again, in a lonesome voice:

> *Clap hands, clap hands,*
> *Till Daddy comes home.*
> *Daddy's got money*
> *And Mummy's got none.*

Clap hands, clap hands,
Till Daddy comes home.
Daddy's got money
And Mummy's got none

And then all the children started singing the song, too, including the quiet girl who never spoke. And Amy sat there, watching Katrina, whose eyes were closed now, and the nursery suddenly felt very small.

Friday nights were always the worst for taxis, and that night Amy got a dozen phone calls.

'I'm sorry,' she said to one guy whose voice sounded familiar, 'but you've got the wrong number.'

'No, no, I'm sorry,' he said. 'It's just I'm stuck and don't know what to do.'

The man kept calling, saying he was stuck and didn't know what to do. She asked him to stop, but the calls kept coming, until the man finally admitted that he was the fake plumber, the one who'd come around with his kid.

'It was a strange time,' he said. 'And I'm still trying to work it all out. Can I come over to you?'

'When?' she said.

'Will you be in in the next hour?'

The electric tripped then, the lights went out. Amy could hear Rhys calling from upstairs.

'It's late,' she told the man. 'And the electric's just gone.'

'I'm good with electrics,' he said.

'I don't think—'

'Please,' he said. 'I just need to be in that bathroom again. I want to understand what was going on in my head.'

'You what?' she said.

'I reckon I'm going mad,' he said. 'And if I could just see that bathroom again, I might be able to make sense of things. Otherwise, something bad is gonna happen to me. I can feel it.'

'Oh,' she said.

And there, in the hall in the dark, Amy had to agree: opportunities rarely knock, chances for change are few and far between, but disaster – sweet stupid disaster – always finds its way.

BIG PIT

When I met Emily from the bus station, her face looked squashed and bloated. She was overweight, carrying a red Head sports bag, and if she hadn't been my sister I would have assumed she was someone I'd never speak to, would have no need to speak to. She gave me an awkward wave and walked over to the car. I went to hug her but she said, 'No, no.'

On the way back to mine, she pointed at the tourists by the castle. A Japanese man in *Jurassic Park* get-up was arranging his family for a photograph.

'You know,' she said, 'I've never met a Japanese person. Why do you think they come here?'

'I dunno,' I said. 'But I doubt there's many castles in Japan.'

She bit a fingernail, and rotated the finger to yank it off. I noticed the skin on her face – her cheeks, her forehead – was blotchy and flaking. Her hair was shiny with grease.

'I see,' she said, and she kept looking out the window, at the Japanese family with their thumbs aloft. She exhaled an over-the-top sigh and looked at me. 'Why aren't you wearing your glasses?'

I told her about the laser surgery, and she whistled sarcastically.

'Wow,' she said. 'How the other half live.'

When I showed her to the spare room, she threw her bag on the floor, inspected the sofa bed, then lay down. She looked around, at the curtains, at the ceiling. She was silent for a few moments, then she said, 'I know people always say it'll only be a few days. But it really only will be a few days.'

In Nando's she ordered spicy chicken wings and I watched as she nibbled around the edges and wiped her hands every minute with baby wipes.

'How's work going?' I said.

'Shit.'

'How long you got off?'

'Two weeks. I got a doctor's note. She says I have "severe stress" and "free-floating anxiety". I don't think I should take all the days, though. That'd just give them another reason to get rid of me.'

A waitress passed, and Emily grabbed her by the elbow. The waitress was young and attractive – dark hair and pale skin.

'Do you know where you get the chickens from?' Emily asked.

The waitress ran a finger across her eye, as if removing some dust or a hair. 'The freezer,' she said.

Emily smiled. 'A straight answer,' she said. 'I haven't had one of them in months.'

Back at mine I offered Emily a beer, but she declined – she said it didn't mix well with the tablets. I made her a tea, and we watched Chelsea v Barcelona on the telly. She had been a Chelsea fan all her life, and whenever there was a bad foul or a good shot I'd look at her, hoping to see some sort of reaction. She only seemed to get agitated with the camerawork though.

'Why do they always have to do close-ups when the ball goes out to the wing?' she said. 'I want to see the game. I want to see the strikers, I want to see the midfielders breaking into the box.'

I was getting tired and my eyes were drying out, so I kept juicing them with the eye drops. When the game ended, and the adverts came on, Emily said she'd have an early night. And though I had work to get up for, I stayed up late, and took out the photos that Mum had given me a few months back. Photos of me and Emily as kids. From the age of eleven, Emily began to hold herself oddly – all slumped and shifty – as if she didn't know how to be. Mum blamed the secondary school. She said that Emily had been a confident kid until she made the move up. I'd never really believed that, but looking at the pictures again, I started to understand what Mum had meant – Emily looked so lost in the teenage ones. But maybe that was just because she was a teenager. Who's to say?

*

She was already up by the time I came down for breakfast. She was perched on the sofa, drinking coffee and watching the news.

'Plans for the day?' I said.

'Solicitor's.'

'Need a lift?'

'No, no,' she said. 'I think I'm capable of catching a bus. Could I borrow your laptop, though?'

I handed it to her, got ready for work, gave her the spare key, then headed for the door.

'If you need anything—'

'I'll call my little brother,' she said. 'My big protective little brother.'

And she did: three times in the first hour. She called to ask how the shower worked, how to turn the heating on, and whether the beeping noise coming from the attic was normal (it wasn't).

'When's the solicitor meeting?' I asked.

'Oh, I got it wrong,' she said. 'It's tomorrow. I'm just gonna take some time out, I think. Have a relax, you know?'

At work, I was caught up with a campaign that had been going on for months. An old guy called Bryn Beynon had won £346,000 on the lottery and asked us to design giant posters to promote the Welsh language. He had never learned Welsh himself, but his grandmother had spoken it to him as a kid, and now he wanted to 'make a difference'. He planned to put the posters on billboards and bus shelters up and down the Rhymney Valley. But he kept changing his mind as to what he actually wanted, and he came into the office every week with new photos of scenery he thought we should use, or examples of Celtic designs he really liked. I'd tell him to just get his daughter to email me the stuff, but he always insisted on coming in.

'I'll be buggered if we did that,' he said. 'You never know who's looking at them emails.'

I actually quite liked his visits. I used to pretend to the other guys in the office that he did my head in, but Bryn was just lovely. He was the one who paid for my laser eye surgery. He was too scared to have the procedure done himself – he was convinced the lasers would leave him blind – but he insisted I get it done, and insisted that he pay. I tried for ages to talk him out of it, but he wouldn't take no for an answer. He even threatened to cancel the design contract if I didn't get the surgery. And it wasn't as if he was saying that to show off or anything – no one else in the office knew about it.

Emily's first morning at the house, Bryn was in the office again, explaining his latest idea. It centred on the character of a skateboarding kid who wore baggy jeans, a sideward-facing hat, and a T-shirt with a C emblazoned on it. The C, Bryn proudly told me, stood for both Cymraeg and 'cool'. He'd even sketched it for me on some very nice tracing paper.

'Based it on my grandson, I did,' he said. He took off his milk-bottle glasses and wiped them with a yellow chamois.

'Bryn,' I said, 'I think you're onto a winner.'

At his desk, Steve raised a finger-gun to his own head, pulled the trigger.

Bryn started talking about his family again then, about how his son was a natural at golf, and how his daughter had worked so hard to become a primary-school teacher. He told me about his dead Uncle Tom who wasn't really his uncle, and all the years he, Bryn, had worked in the Peter's Pie factory in Bedwas.

'I was lucky,' he said. 'You know, I used to work down the mines. Started when I was fourteen, I did. But when I was seventeen I got an ear infection. It got all swollen and pus-y and it bloody hurt every time I swallowed or moved my head. So after a few weeks I finally went, *right, that's it, I hafta go to the doctor.* So I went to the doctor and he said, *Bryn, you've got a bloody big build-up of wax in there*, so he put a needle in but he bloody shot through and burst my effin eardrum.'

'That must have hurt,' I said.

'Aye,' he said. 'I knew straight away something was up. Like my head was under water, it was. Anyway, to cut a long story short, I couldn't work down the mines after that – it was against the regulations. So I worked in the payroll department for twenty-odd years, and in 1986 I ended up at Peter's Pies. When d'you think you'll get this poster done?'

'Leave it with me,' I said.

'Good good,' he said. 'And I want them massive, alright? So you can read them from the road. If you're driving, I mean.'

'I know what you mean, Bryn,' I said, and I showed him the designs I'd prepped already. He asked me to zoom in and in, until the images were up to 300 per cent.

'Seriously,' he said, twiddling his glasses. 'My bloody eyesight.'

'You should get the surgery,' I said. 'It's really nothing. It's just like someone blowing into your eyes. It doesn't even last a second.'

'Ah, I couldn't,' he said. He leaned his head in at the screen to get a better look. 'It's not worth the risk.'

He studied the images as I clicked through them on the computer: male-voice choirs on mountaintops, castles with Welsh flags, and rugby players making crunching tackles. The usual stuff, but it was what he wanted.

'You're doing a great job,' he said, straightening back up. 'Is there anything else I can do for you now?'

'I'm alright, Bryn,' I said.

'You sure?' he said, and then he whispered, 'You sure you don't need a bitta cash for anything else?'

'No, no,' I said, 'you've been too good to me already.'

He slipped me a twenty-quid note on his way out. He told me to treat my girlfriend.

*

When I got back, Emily wasn't in. There was just a note on the living-room table: *The laptop was making a funny noise so I'm taking it to be repaired. Didn't want to bother you with any more calls. I'll see you later.*

The laptop had all my freelance projects on it. And years of work and ideas I'd never got round to backing up. I called Emily but her phone was off. So I went to the only computer shop in town – a small dingy place on Bartlett Street – and sure enough my sister was sitting down next to the counter, chatting away with the guy who worked there.

'Is it okay?' I said. 'The laptop?'

'The successful brother,' she said, pointing at me. And the computer man laughed like it was some in-joke.

'Is the laptop alright?'

'She's saved you a fortune, mate,' the guy said. 'The fan was buggered and the hard drive was overheating. It all would have packed in any minute if she hadn't have brought it in.'

My sister smiled.

'When I heard it making that noise, I thought *that's not normal*,' she said. 'It sounded like a dying horse. *That's not normal*, I thought. And that's why I brought it here.'

'Are my files still on it though?'

'It's all good, mate,' the guy said. 'All safe and sound.'

'Thank God,' I said. 'Thank you.' I asked how much I owed, but he said not to worry – he'd had a good time with my sister.

'She's a great laugh,' he said. 'And that's a rare thing for a woman.'

We stayed up late that night. I wanted to go to bed, but Emily was in the mood for sharing. Talking about Pete, her husband, she'd get angry and raise her voice.

'I'm not Pete,' I said. 'You don't have to shout at me.'

'But you don't *get it*,' she said. 'You're *all* the same.'

I knew the trajectory the conversation would take. How it would move from Pete to men in general, and then back to Dad, as if *he* were the primordial soup from which all the shit in the world originated.

My eyes felt strained and bloodshot, like I'd been sat in front of the computer for twenty hours. As Emily spoke it was as if all the moisture in the air was evaporating, and my sockets were being wrung out.

'Dad always treated you differently,' she said. 'Just because you're a boy. I've spoken about this with—'

'Can we not?' I said.

'You hated him more than I did,' she said.

'I know,' I said. 'But I don't like to go to bed wound up.'

'Have a drink then,' she said.

'I've got work tomorrow,' I said. I looked at my watch. It was gone twelve. 'Actually, I'm in work today.'

'And I've got to be up to see the solicitor,' she said. 'But come on, it's been five years. Fifteen hundred days.'

She climbed off the couch and went to the kitchen. She came back with two cans.

'I thought you're not meant to drink with the tablets,' I said.

'Fuck it,' she said, handing me a can. 'One won't do no harm.'

She settled back down on the couch, and opened my laptop. Within a minute, Dolly Parton's 'Jolene' was playing.

'Is this the *Greatest Tits*?' I said.

'Nope.' She shook her head. 'It's *The Breast Of*. What will we toast to?'

I tapped a rhythm on my can. 'To dead fathers?'

She opened her beer. 'Bit morbid. How about to family in general?'

'Yeah, alright,' I said. 'A toast to family in general.'

Neither of us could be arsed to move, so we settled for air-toasting. Then Emily started talking about the summer of 1992. I was seven and she was ten, and we stayed with Aunt Sarah and our cousin Rob. We had watched the entire Barcelona Olympics on a sofa bed in the living room, sleeping out there at night. Growing up, we told each other the story so many times that my memories of the reminiscing became stronger than the summer itself.

'And you kept drawing Edd the Duck in a headband!' she said.

'Yeah, and Rob kept wanting to use the sofa bed for a high-jump competition!'

In a film we'd have gone quiet then, and silently considered Rob, who died at fourteen from blood poisoning. But we talked about Dad instead. Maybe it was a subliminal thing that took us there, like when you hear a phrase on telly, then start humming a tune to a song with the same words.

'The more I think about it the more I think Dad was actually mental,' I said, and I took a big sip of my can. 'What with the hygiene stuff and all that.'

'Yeah. Well, it'd explain where I get it from.'

'Ah, I didn't mean it like that,' I said.

'It's okay,' she said, then she laughed. 'I'm officially mental. I've got the doctor's note to prove it an' all.'

'I'm sorry,' I said.

'It's okay,' she said. 'He fucked us both up.'

I'd been thinking a lot about Dad since meeting Bryn. Dad had hated the Welsh language and even banned us from speaking it in the house. When I asked him why he sent us to a Welsh school if he felt so strongly about it, all he said was: 'It was your mother's decision.'

'Do you worry about becoming like him?' Emily said. She was lying back on the couch now, her feet hanging over the edge. From where I was sitting I could see the brown dead skin, the calluses. Dad hated feet. Women's feet especially. He used to insist that Emily wore socks in the house at all times.

'Not really,' I said, and I got up. 'I sometimes see parts of him in me, but – actually, do you wannanother can?'

'I wouldn't say no,' she said.

'Do you ever wonder why he was so cruel, though?' I was paused in the doorway. 'There's an old guy I'm doing design work for, and he's just lovely. Why couldn't we have had a dad like that?'

Emily stretched her arms, then rested her hands atop her head.

'Mam's fault, I suppose,' she said. 'She's the one who married the man. Actually, how do you find Mam these days? She's getting odd, I reckon.'

'I know,' I said, and I went into kitchen. I looked in the fridge and thought of Mum. Then I carried a four-pack out to the living room. 'I think she's just lonely,' I said, and handed Emily a can. On the laptop, Dolly was singing about her coat of many colours.

'Yeah, maybe,' Emily said. 'Does she talk much about Dad with you?'

I watched her take a sip, then tap a rhythm on her drink. I wondered if the tapping habit was hereditary.

'No,' I said. 'Funnily enough, she doesn't bring him up.'

Emily put her can down on the carpet then. 'I know we've had this out before—'

'Do we have to?' I said.

'I just don't understand why you didn't come. It was *one* day. Even for Mam's sake, couldn't you have spent just one *hour*—?'

'Please,' I said.

She put her hands out in apology.

'You're right,' she said. 'You're right. I'm sorry. I'll leave it.'

She started talking about Pete again, and I asked if she was sure it was over.

'Ah yeah,' she said, picking at her sleeve. 'It's done done done.'

She nodded a few times, closed her eyes, then hummed the chorus to 'D–I–V–O–R–C–E'.

'So, tomorrow,' I said. 'You worried about seeing the solicitor?'

'Nah,' she said, and she sat up. 'I know what I've got to say and do. There's nothing more to it really.'

'I am sorry,' I said. 'You know, I really thought—'

'Yeah, me too,' she said.

Two hours and six cans later, we had our arms around each other singing 'I Will Always Love You'.

*

I called in sick the next day. I didn't want to leave Emily alone in the house, and I thought she might need some support with the solicitor. But she came out of the shower looking like a new person, almost glowing, like she was ready to take control of things. She insisted she was fine to go in on her own, so I dropped her off outside the office and went to a pharmacy to pick up more ointment. My eyes were stinging raw, and felt like they'd been scratched with hay. I sat in the car and applied the drops until the itch felt wet.

I thought about calling Mum, to let her know that Emily and I were talking again. But I couldn't face the questions, and the over-serious tone that Mum always adopted whenever she spoke about Emily. After Dad died, Mum was diagnosed with depression, and suddenly saw depression in everyone around her. If I told her I was tired, she'd tell me to see a doctor. If I told her I was annoyed by something, she'd tell me to seek counselling. Show her a Magic Eye poster and she'd see a manic-depressed donkey in need of 'some time out'.

An hour after I'd dropped her off, I called Emily but she didn't answer. So I went to the solicitors, a tiny little place above the hairdressers. The office smelled of mould, and the white lace curtains seemed to have coffee stains on them. A fax machine chugged out paper. When I asked the secretary about my sister, she called the solicitor out – a small, thin man with dyed black hair, who emerged from behind a red door.

'She was only here five minutes,' he said. 'She told me to give everything to her husband.'

'Shit,' I said.

'I told her it wasn't wise,' he said, 'but she wasn't listening.'

I drove around looking for Emily, and kept calling her phone. I drove around some more then headed home.

When I got back, she was sitting on the couch with a Japanese girl. They were playing Mario Kart.

'This is Sumiko,' she said, pausing the game. 'We met down by the castle.' My sister pretended to take photos in the air. 'She was snap, snap, snapping away, and we got talking.'

The girl gave me a little wave. She was pretty and delicate-looking, as if she'd been drawn with a thin-nib pencil. She looked about twelve.

'Hi,' I said, waving back. 'Just a minute,' and I ushered Emily into the kitchen.

'Where the hell did you go?' I said.

'Back here, obviously.'

'Fuck's sake,' I said. 'I was—'

'Well, I'm fine,' she said, scratching her face. Her ears were red and raw, and bits of white skin, like tiny pastry flakes, were peeling from where she'd dug in her nails.

'How old's that girl?' I said. 'Where's her family?'

'Calm heads,' she said. 'She's a student. On exchange.'

'Right.'

'She's studying molecular science in Cardiff. She's probably twenty-something.'

'Okay,' I said. 'Are you okay?'

'I'm fine,' she said. 'I told Sumiko I'd give her a tour of the valleys, though. The Big Pit and all that.'

'What? How you going to do that?'

'In a motor vehicle. Yours, most probably.'

'You want the car?'

'Well,' she said, wiping her hands with the baby wipes, 'I can't really drive at the moment.'

'How come?'

'My nerves have gone. I keep thinking I've run people over.'

'Right.'

'I have to keep going back every twenty metres to check. It takes me ten bloody hours to get anywhere.'

We drove up the valley and over to Blaenavon, the two of them sitting in the back – my sister commentating and lying the whole way.

'Formed by a glacier,' she said, pointing at a mountain in Abersychan, and making wild gestures in the air. 'Big ice, you know?'

'Ahh,' Sumiko said, politely, 'yesss. Big.'

'Biggest mountain in Wales,' my sister said.

'Really?'

'Yep,' Emily said, nodding sagely. 'Very big mountain.'

I hadn't been to the Big Pit since I was a kid. But the place hadn't changed – it was still manned by former miners, still grimy, and I felt the dust in the air as soon we got in. I paid the entry for us all, and the guide, a guy in his sixties with a solid face, dressed us up in the gear: a white helmet with a lamp, a big heavy belt he clamped each of us in, and attached to it something he called a 'self-rescuer' – a little tub with up to an hour's worth of oxygen.

'In case we get trapped down there,' Emily explained to Sumiko, groping her own neck and pretending to gasp for air.

There were only six of us on the tour. A couple in their fifties, an Indian man on his own, and us three. The guide took us into the old steel cage of a lift and we dropped, very slowly, three hundred feet underground.

'Did you work in this pit?' my sister asked as we rattled our way down.

'Aye,' said the guide. 'A good pit. Here for ten years, I was.'

'What was it like?' asked the woman in her fifties.

'Back-breaking,' said the guide. 'And so hot all the time. And so dark. It was rewarding work, though.'

The woman nodded.

'My father worked down the mine,' she said. 'Died of emphysema in the end. Tough, tough work.'

'I'm sorry to hear that,' the miner said. And the woman's husband, a big man, put a hand on her shoulder.

The guide showed us the pit, asked us to touch the walls, and described how difficult it could be to get the coal out. I needed to rub my eyes – I could feel all the bits of dust in there, settling behind the balls.

'In a minute I'll ask you to turn off your lamps,' the guide said. 'And then you'll experience a kind of darkness like nothing else.'

We walked on a bit, my sister urging Sumiko to take photos. Then the guide gave us a countdown from five and we switched off our lamps. And he hadn't lied: we couldn't see a thing, not even our own hands.

'Imagine,' he said. 'You're down here and your lamp

goes out. You walk along, touching the walls, but you've got no idea how far you've gone, and you don't know where the exit is.'

'Very scary,' said Sumiko, and everyone *mmm*'d in agreement.

'Yeah,' said the guide. 'And spare a thought for the first miners to work down here. When this pit was built back in 1810, the miners didn't have lamps like you and me have. They carried open flames. But coal dust collects firedamp – a collection of gases. And one of those gases is methane. And you can guess what happens when a build-up of methane meets a flame . . .'

I brought my hand close to my face and touched my nose. I put my hand to my pocket, just to feel my phone. The guide told us about the Senghenydd disaster in 1913. There was an explosion at 8 a.m., and that explosion disrupted the coal dust on the floor, which clouded up and itself exploded, which disrupted more dust, which caused more explosions. And so on. And on. Over four hundred men died in one morning. The guide told us that the total compensation amounted to £24, about a sixpence for every life.

The tour seemed longer than I remembered. When we got back to the car the interior was hot. We wound the windows down, and the smell of cow shit swept in. The hill roads were narrow, and sheep clung to the sides, lying down at impossible inclines. My eyes felt on fire now, and I was driving with one hand on the wheel, with the other squeezing the drops into my eyes. I came very close to hitting a sheep, but managed to swerve just in time.

'Bad luck,' Sumiko said. 'Bad luck to crash sheep.'

I pulled over and slapped my face a bit, then put on a Bob Dylan mix I'd made. And though they were blurry to me, the hill roads unfurled in calmness then, as Bob sung 'One Too Many Mornings' to us all in the car.

'Do you know, Sumiko,' I heard Emily say in the back, 'the word for sheep in Welsh is *defaid*. Can you say that? *Dev-ide*.'

'Div-ide?'

'Almost,' said my sister. But it's *dev*-ide. Dev, dev—'

'Div-ide?' said Sumiko again.

'Not bad!' said Emily. 'You'll be fluent in a week.'

Sumiko laughed, and the two of them carried on talking while I tuned out to thoughts of Bryn and his giant billboards. His ultimate plan, he had told me, was to get someone to build a ten-foot mechanical dragon that would walk the length and breadth of the country, spitting out Welsh dictionaries to children.

Of course, there was no doubting that the man was deranged. But I liked Bryn a lot. He was genuinely kind, and he'd found something he thought worth doing. He told me that he'd worked too hard all his life – sometimes doing sixty hours a week – but that he'd done it for his kids. And now, looking back, he regretted not seeing them more when they were growing up. But having retired and won all that money, he couldn't wait to spend time with his children, his grandkids, and Sue, his wife.

When he died a few weeks later – a heart attack as he was getting out of the bath – it hit me harder than it should have. It's like it opened a valve, and all the feelings about Dad and my cousin came back and started clogging me up. I designed the funeral's order of service though: a photo of Bryn and his grandson Owain on the cover. Owain with his teenage emo fringe covering his eyes, and Bryn with his milk-bottle glasses, and the two of them with a Peter's Pie in their hands. I didn't make it to the funeral, but his daughter told me it had been a good send-off.

*

We made our way back into Caerphilly, and the rush-hour traffic, and my sister told me to take a right at the roundabout.

'What for?' I said.

'Sumiko wants to go to B&Q.'

'Does she now?' I said. 'And what does Sumiko want in B&Q? A bit of decking?'

'She wants to show us something,' Emily said.

'What?'

Emily leaned forward and whispered: 'Small trees.'

I parked the car and we went into B&Q. My sister pointed towards the outdoor garden and Sumiko raced ahead.

'She's great, isn't she?' said Emily, and we quickly scuttled to dodge a bald man carrying a large plank.

'Look,' I said. 'Can we sit down and talk properly later?'

'About what?'

'About you leaving the house to Pete. You can't just walk away from it like that. We'll take Sumiko home after this, okay? And then we'll talk things over?'

She nodded slowly, as if she was registering each word in her head. Then she said, 'Do you think Sumiko can see as much as us? With her eyes and everything.'

I gave Emily a look.

'I'm not being racist,' she said.

'But it's not far off, though, is it?'

'Japanese people have different-shaped eyes,' she said. 'I think it's fair to wonder if that affects their vision.'

'I dunno,' I said.

'I was just thinking about it when we were down the mine.'

I felt my eyes twitching, going dry. 'Seriously,' I said. 'I haven't a clue.'

We moved through the aisles – past blocks of laminate flooring, paint pots and tubes of wallpaper – and went to the outside area. The place was made up like a garden, with green netting enclosing it all. It was hot, and there were loads of tall trees crowded together, flattened at the top from where they hit the meshing. There were garden tables, flowers pots, and different kinds of benches. In the middle, a little fountain flowed. Sumiko was standing there, her hand under the running water. When Emily called out, Sumiko turned and smiled at us.

'Found your bonsai?' asked Emily, her arms open, as if to give Sumiko a hug. Then she moved closer to Sumiko and started staring at her face. I was afraid she was going to make a comment about her eyes, so I took a step forward, as if that would somehow help.

Sumiko shook her head. 'No bonsai,' she said, and Emily kept staring at her. She got right up to her face, like she was inspecting the pores. Sumiko looked at me, and all I could do was nothing. Then Emily reached into her bag and pulled out the baby wipes.

'Coal dust,' Emily said, and there was a bite to her voice. 'Firedamp.'

I looked closer at Sumiko, and I could see a small wisp of black glistening on her cheek. With the baby wipes, Emily began swiping at Sumiko's face. It was so awkward I couldn't watch. I closed my eyes and put my head in my hands. And seeing the dark of nothing, I remembered how dark it had been down the mine. I thought about the explosion at Senghenydd, and I imagined all the women on the doorsteps, whole streets of other-century women in front of their houses, eyes peeled to the end of the road, their heads lifted, watching the smoke billow from the pit. All those funerals, all those days of black. A thing like that would surely never leave you.

When I opened my eyes, Sumiko had her hands out and was telling Emily to stop, to please stop, but Emily was gripping her shoulder, and she kept wiping, kept rubbing hard at Sumiko's face. I stepped in and grabbed Emily by the arms, trying to hold her back. But she was crying, her whole body seemed to shake.

'You heard the Big Pit man, too,' she said. 'One spark and this could all just blow.'

ALL THE BOYS

The best man won't tell them it's Dublin until they get to Bristol Airport. He'll tell them to bring euros and don't bother packing shorts. The five travelling from Caerphilly will drink on the minibus. And Big Mike, the best man, will spend the first twenty minutes reading and rereading the A4 itinerary he typed up on MS Word. The plastic polypocket will be wedged thick with flight tickets and hostel reservations. It will be crumpled and creased from the constant hand-scrunching and metronome swatting against his suitcase – the only check-in bag on the entire trip. He'll spend the journey to the airport telling Gareth, and anyone who listens, that Rob had better never marry again, that he couldn't handle the stress of organising another one of these.

'You should see my desk in work,' Big Mike will say. 'It's covered in notes for this fuckin stag. It's been like a full-time job.'

Gareth will nod and Gareth will sympathise. He'll just be glad to get out of Caerphilly for the weekend; he's been waiting months for this, has imagined how it all might go. He'll take a swig of his can, and look to Rob's father. Rob's father will be fifty-four in two weeks and will think there's something significant about the fact, about being twice the age of his son. He had two kids and a house by the time he was twenty-seven, and he'll think about that as he listens to Larry telling the story about the woman he picked up at the Kings. She'd taken Larry back to her place, and in the middle of the night he'd heard sex noises coming from the room next to hers. Larry said to the woman, 'Your housemate's a bit wild', and the woman replied, 'I don't have a housemate, love. That's my daughter.'

Hucknall and Peacock, travelling from London, will arrive at Bristol before the others. They'll sit in the bar getting drunk and studying departures screens. Hucknall will have spent the whole morning moaning about the fact they're flying from Bristol, and why couldn't Big Mike have just told them where they're going?

'Bet you it's Dublin,' Hucknall will say, leaning back in his chair, his knees spread wide, his hands smoothing his tan chinos. 'Bet Big Mike's too scared to book somewhere foreign.'

'Don't make a difference to me,' Peacock will say. 'I'll clear up wherever we go.'

When the Caerphilly boys join the now-London ones at the airport bar, Big Mike will confirm that it's Dublin they're headed to. And he'll loudly declare the weekend's drinking rule: pints must always be held in the left hand. If you find yourself holding two drinks, your own drink must be in your left hand. Failure to adhere will result in a forfeit, as decided by Lead Ruler Larry. The boys will all say that's easy, and start suggesting additional rules, but Big Mike will be defiant: the left-hand rule is king.

'You sure no one here's a secret leftie, though?' Hucknall will ask.

'I've done my research,' Big Mike will say. 'Rob's dad is left-footed, but he's definitely right-handed. I made him write his name out earlier.'

When Peacock – with perfect stubble and coiffed hair – goes to the airport bar, everyone will laugh at his shoes that seem to be made of straw.

'Couldn't believe it when I met him at Paddington,' Hucknall will say. 'Doesn't he look benter than a horseshoe?'

'I've seen straighter semicircles,' Rob will say.

Gareth will shout to Peacock: 'Mate, why don't you do yourself a favour and just come out?'

Peacock will stand there, between table and bar, and kiss his own biceps. He'll accept the jibes, and say none of the boys has any idea about style. He'll take the piss out of Caerphilly's clothes shops, and say David Beckham wore a pair of shoes just like these to the *Iron Man 3* premiere. And that will be it: Peacock will be called Iron Man Three for the rest of the trip.

When they board the plane, Larry will tell the air

stewardess that Peacock's ticket isn't valid, that his name is Iron Man Three.

When they get to the hostel in Temple Bar – and Hucknall has finally stopped going on about the ten-minute wait for Big Mike's suitcase, he'll ask if Iron Man Three has a reservation.

And in Fitzsimons on the first night, to every girl that Peacock talks to, one of the boys will come up and say, 'Don't bother, Iron Man's gay.'

Peacock will laugh. 'They're just jealous,' he'll tell the girl from Minneapolis or Wexford or Rome. 'They wouldn't know fashion if it woke them up in the morning and gave them a little kiss.'

Gareth, meanwhile, will be at the bar ordering shots. He'll have his arm around Rob and he'll tell him that he loves him, that he's really happy he's happy. He'll make Rob do shots with him – sambuca, whiskey and vodka – and Rob will say he can't handle any more after the apple sours.

'Who's for shots?' Gareth will say, looking around 'Shotiau?'

He'll order shots for whoever's beside him at the bar. He'll buy randomers shots. And he'll persuade the English barman to have a shot with him. He's not meant to, but he'll do one just to shut Gareth up.

At a table, Rob's father will have his arm around his son.

'I love Rachel, you know,' Rob will say, his eyes ablaze. 'I really love her.'

'Just pace yourself,' his father will say quietly. 'The boys are getting wrecked. They won't even notice if you don't drink the stuff they're giving you.'

He'll offer to drink his son's drinks; he'll get wasted so that his son may be saved.

Big Mike will be careering around the pub making sure everyone's alright. He'll always have a pint in his left hand. And he'll be going from boy to boy, just to make sure everyone's okay. This first night he'll be torn between keeping steady and getting absolutely bollocksed. He'll decide on ordering half-pints but asking the barman to pour them into pint glasses.

'Dun want anyone thinking I'm gay,' he'll say, and he'll order another pint for Rob, and place it down at his table without saying a word.

And Larry? He'll be getting attacked by an English girl for calling her sugar-tits. When her friends pull her off, he'll retouch his hair and say, 'Fair play, my dear, that was lovely. Can we do that back at yours?'

The night will become an ungodly mess. All the boys will be pouncing on each other for holding pints in their right hand, and drinking shots as forfeits, and drinking faster as the night slips by. They'll make moves on girls on hen-do's from Brighton and Bangor and Mayo. By eleven, Hucknall will be puking in the corner of the dance floor, and Rob's father, after a quiet word in Big

Mike's ear, will take Rob back to the hostel. Peacock will go missing, talking to some girl somewhere, his deep V-neck shirt showing off his tonely chest and glimmering sunbed tan. And Rob, the groom (lest we forget), will be flat-out on the hostel bed, fully clothed, but shoeless, his father having taken them off while his drunken twenty-seven-year-old son lay half-comatose. He'll send a text to the boy's mother: '*all gd here, back at the hostel. Rob's safe and asleep.*'

Outside McDonald's, Larry'll coax the boys to take turns hugging the Polish dwarf in a leprechaun costume.

Larry will say: 'Cracking job this would be for you, Mikey-boy.'

Big Mike will laugh and grab at his own hair. He'll slur, 'I'm small. I know I'm small. But at least I'm *not* fucking ginger.'

Gareth will ask the Polish dwarf if Big Mike can try on his hat, but the man will decline.

'No hat, no job,' he'll say.

So they'll take turns to photograph each other hugging the Polish dwarf in a leprechaun costume. They'll ask a passer-by to take photos of them hugging the Polish dwarf in a leprechaun costume. And when the Polish man points at the little pot-of-gold money box and asks for two euro, Larry will say – actually, Larry won't say anything the leprechaun will understand. Larry will be speaking Welsh. When abroad, all the boys slag everyone in Welsh.

At Zaytoon, Gareth, Big Mike and Larry will queue for food while Hucknall sits on the pavement outside, his head arched between his legs, his vomit softly coating the curb and cobblestones like one of Dali's melted clocks. A blonde girl will ask the boys if they're from Wales. She'll say she loves the accent, and Larry will say he likes hers too – where's she from? But when she answers, she'll be looking at Gareth, not Larry. She'll say she likes his quiff.

'Cheers,' Gareth will say. 'I grew it myself.'

She'll be asking about the tattoo of a fish on Gareth's arm when Larry will tell her that Gareth has a girlfriend called Carly, that they're buying together a house in Ystrad Mynach. The girl will lose interest, not immediately – she won't be that obvious – but she'll allow herself to be pulled back into the gravitational force of her friends who lean against the restaurant window.

'Cheers,' Gareth will say to Larry. 'You're such a twat.'

'Any time,' Larry will say. 'Have you seen *Iron Man Three*?'

Big Mike will have his hands on the glass counter, his head resting like a small bundle in his arms. Gareth will be looking at Big Mike's tiny little frame, his tiny little shoes against the base of the counter, and Gareth will think he should text Carly back.

'I ain't seen Peacock all night,' he'll say. 'Probably shagging some bloke somewhere.'

Larry will smile. 'Aye,' he'll say. 'Wouldn't surprise me.'

all the boys

Saturday, the hostel room smelling like sweated alcohol and men, heavy tongues will wake stuck to the roofs of dry mouths. Set up a microphone, and this is what you'll hear: waking-up farts and morning groans; zips and unzips on mini-suitcases and sports bags; the library-*shhhhhhh* of Lynx sprays; and the sounds of the bathroom door opening and slamming, its lock rotating clockwise in the handle. Pop your nose through the door, and this is what you'll smell: dehydrated shit mingling with the minty hostel shower gel in the hot, steamy air. And back in the room, more sounds now: the beginning of last night's stories, the where-did-you-go-tos, the how-the-hell-did-I-get-backs and Larry inviting the boys to guess if the skin he's pulling over his boxers belongs to his cock or balls.

Big Mike will be first to breakfast, the others dripping behind. All the boys will be scrolling through iPhones for photos from last night, with Rob's father doing the same on his digital camera. There'll be sympathetic bleats for headaches and wrenched stomachs, with para-cetamol handed around like condiments. Big Mike will be urging the boys to get a move on or they'll never make it to Croke Park. Hucknall will ask why the hell are they going there anyway? And Big Mike, tapping the inventory in its polypocket, will say: 'Culture, mate. Culture.' Fried breakfasts and questions: how's an Irish breakfast different to an English? When you buying the house then, Gareth? And seriously, Peacock, where the hell did you end up last night?

Peacock's story will be confusing and confused. He got in a taxi with a girl, and she was well up for it – he was fingering her in the backseat. ('Backseat?' Larry'll say. 'Up the arse, like?' and Peacock will go, 'No, the back-seat of the taxi, you dickwad.') Anyway, when they got to her place she realised she didn't have her keys ('Sure this wasn't a bloke?' Rob will say.) So Peacock and the girl walked for like an hour to somewhere – Cadbra or some random place – and when they arrived she told him he couldn't come in because it was her nan's house. She just went in and closed the door on him. When he finally found a taxi, he didn't have enough cash so the driver dropped him off at some random ATM in a 24-hour shop, but Peacock got talking to some random guy about London for ages ('Oh yeah, bet you did,' Gareth'll say) and when he came out, the taxi had gone, so he – ('He's holding his glass in his right hand!' Rob's father will say. 'It's orange juice,' Peacock will say. 'It don't matter,' Larry will say. 'Down it!') – so he found the tram stop and —

'Gay Boy Robert Downey Junior,' Hucknall will say. 'I'm bored now. Worst Man, when we going to Croke Park?'

Big Mike will be glaring. He'll say: 'As soon as you've finished your fucking breakfast.'

All the boys will be surprised and impressed by Croke Park's size, by the vastness of the changing rooms, the way the training centre gleams. When the guide takes them out onto the edge of the pitch, he'll point to the stand at the far end, and tell them about the Bloody Sunday Massacre in 1920, how the British army opened fire on the crowd during a Gaelic football match. Fourteen were killed, he'll say. Two players were shot. There'll be a silence. Rob's father will be nodding – he'll have read about all this in the guide book he bought at the Centra in Temple Bar. Three of the boys will be wearing Man Utd shirts. And the guide will go on, explaining how Gaelic football and hurling – he'll just call it GAA, and it'll take a few minutes for the boys to fully get what he's talking about – are not sports, but expressions of resistance. But they're also more than that, they're not just reactive things. It's in the blood, he'll say. And Gareth will be sort of startled. Something the guide says, something of its tone, will resonate. Though resonate isn't quite how Gareth would put it; he won't even know what he's thinking. He'll just be looking out to the far stand, trying to picture how it all happened.

'They were boys,' the guide will say. 'The ones who fought for independence, they were younger than all you.'

The sky will be white, and there'll be silence and rapture. When the guide leaves them at the museum, Hucknall will say to the boys, 'Fucking hell, I thought he'd never shut up.'

And Larry will put on an Irish accent and go: '*GAA is in the blood.*'

And Hucknall will laugh and go: '*And they killed all our boys* . . . Yeah, nice one, Worst Man. Most depressing stag do in the world. You got any other crap trips in that suitcase of yours?'

Big Mike will be quiet, he won't know what to say.

'I enjoyed it,' Rob will say, and his father will thank Big Mike for bringing them.

Gareth will send a text to Carly. '*Miss you too*', it'll say.

Peacock will be using his iPhone to check his hair.

They'll get a taxi back into town, then they'll walk around and look at things. Larry'll be in hysterics when he sees the place called Abrakebabra, insisting that one of the boys take his photo next to the sign. They'll walk in a group, taking up half the width of Westmoreland Street, wondering what the hell goes on in the massive white building with the huge columns that look as if they belong in Rome.

'It's a bank,' Rob's father will say, and Big Mike will go, 'No wonder things are so fucking expensive.'

When they pass Trinity College, Rob's father will say

there's meant to be a nice library in there, he read about it in his guide book. And Gareth will point ahead at Hucknall and Larry as they eye up a group of Spanish-looking tourists, and he'll say: 'I've got a feeling the boys aren't really in the mood for a good read.'

Before they know it, they'll be in Temple Bar again. In Gogarty's they'll order bouquets of Guinness, and Hucknall will insist that they should have gone to the Guinness Factory instead of Croke Park.

Big Mike will say: 'If you know so much, why dun you be fucking best man?' And the boys will do a hand-bags-*oooooh*, and laugh until their already-aching kidneys hurt. A greying man on a guitar will sing 'Whiskey in the Jar' and 'The Wild Rover' ('The Clover song!' Peacock will say), and when the boys request 'Delilah', he'll oblige, and all the boys will sing-shout along, all the while pushing more pints in front of Rob. Rob will be singing loudest now. He'll have decided that tonight's the night he's going to properly go for it. Leaving Croke Park, he'll have felt something stirring, and he'll have told his father he was ready to have one more final night of going nuts.

Gareth will sing along too, but he'll be thinking of his small bedroom at home, of the journey back to Wales tomorrow night.

'By the way,' Big Mike will tell the group when talk turns to eating, 'before we go for food, we've gotta go back to the hostel.'

'How come, Worst Man?' Hucknall will say.

'Costumes for tonight, butt. And if you call me Worst Man one more time I'm gonna knock you out, you ginger prick.'

'Sorry, Worst Man.'

The boys will be awkward-quiet, and Rob's father will ask where they're gonna get the costumes from. And Big Mike will smile now. He'll say, 'Why the hell do you think I checked in a suitcase?'

'A fucking potato?' Hucknall will say. 'Are you fucking serious?'

They'll all be back at their room, and Big Mike will have his suitcase open on the bed, the bag bulging with bumpy, creamy-brown potato costumes.

'Aye,' Big Mike will say. 'Got a problem with that as well, have you?'

Peacock will take a costume from the suitcase and place it over himself in the mirror. 'These gonna make us look fat, you reckon?'

'No way am I wearing a potato costume,' Hucknall will say. 'We're in Ireland, for fuck's sake.'

'Exactly,' Big Mike'll go. 'They love potatoes. *Dirty-tree potatoes.*'

And the boys will shake their heads, will say all sorts.

'Are they all the same size?' Larry'll go.

'All the same,' Big Mike will say, 'except for Rob's. He's wearing something else. Oh, and you all owe me fifteen quid.'

Rob will beam, his teeth visible, a smile in his voice. 'What the fuck you got me?'

A plunging arm into the suitcase depths and Big Mike will pull out something black in cellophane.

Wordless, he'll hand the package to Rob.

Rob will tear at the cellophane. There'll be some kind of dress: green-and-orange and hideous. It'll take a moment for Rob to click: he's been given a woman's Irish dance costume. There'll be white socks to go with it too.

'*Rrrrriverdance!*' Big Mike will scream, doing an odd, high-kneed jig on the hostel floor.

And all the boys will laugh, and Hucknall will say fair play, that's a good un. And once they see that Rob looks the biggest tit, they won't mind dressing up like potatoes. At least we'll all be warm, Rob's father will say.

They'll drink the cans left over from last night, and Gareth will find himself at the point of drunkenness where he wants to fight. He'll offer arm wrestles to everyone. Using Big Mike's suitcase for a table – and at Gareth's insistence – they'll take turns to lie on the floor and arm-wrestle each other. And when he's not competing, Gareth will come up behind Larry, give him a bear hug and lift him off the ground. He'll do the same to Hucknall and Peacock and Rob. They'll be laughing at first, but by the end they'll be properly pushing him off.

In Temple Bar, with the boys dressed like potatoes, and Rob dressed like a female Irish dancer (but wearing his own brown Wrangler boots), they'll argue over where to go for dinner. Foreign girls with dark hair and dinner menus will approach them, trying to coax them into their restaurants. Passers-by will cheer and laugh, and tourists – German, American, Chinese – will ask for photos with all the boys. And they'll begin to get into it, begin to feel like Dublin's central attraction.

'We should start charging,' Larry'll say, as Rob poses for a photo with a girl from Cincinnati. 'Two quid per photo, whadyou reckon?'

At some point in the night someone will say that the euro feels like Monopoly money, and everyone will agree.

After forty minutes of wandering and arguing, they'll land on Dame Street, at an empty Chinese restaurant.

'Never a good sign when it's empty,' Rob's father will say, but they'll have been walking around for too long, and will be too hungry to go elsewhere.

Before they've even ordered, Hucknall will suggest they split the bill. Hucknall is an accountant, Hucknall can afford to say such things. And for reasons beyond them, to save hassle perhaps, everyone will agree. They'll order pints immediately, but the food will take deliberation. They'll all ask each other what they're going to order, as if each boy's afraid of getting the wrong dish, of getting the whole eating-out thing wrong. They'll wind up the waitress who takes their orders, ask her if she'll be joining them for starters, and then they'll make her stand at the table for photos with them all.

The potato costumes will be chunky and clunky, so the chairs will have to be set some distance from the tables, and Gareth will find that to eat he has to lean forward, his back arched like a capital C. His arms will be free, though – he'll have that at least.

'When you buying this place with your missus, then?' Larry will ask.

'We'll see,' Gareth will say, taking a swig of his pint. 'No rush, is there?'

'I heard she wants somewhere by the summer,' Big Mike'll say.

'Carly talks too fucking much,' Gareth will say, and the table will laugh, giddy. Gareth'll say: 'What? It's true. She shouldn't talk about stuff like this with other people. I dun know what's wrong with her.'

Peacock will be smiling like a bag of chips, brimming over, as if he can't believe they're allowed to slag off their partners publicly. He'll think he could handle having a girlfriend if he could just slag her off all the time.

Gareth will finish off his pint and call to the waitress for another. Rob, his arms beginning to itch in the dance dress, will be watching Gareth's left leg. Under the white tablecloth, it'll be shaking.

The boys will chant football songs as they eat. They'll recall stories from school, from holidays, and from other stag trips. And all the boys will laugh as Larry pretends to cry and goes '*I'm soooooo hungry!*' – in imitation of the time Hucknall passed out in Malaga and woke to find his wallet had been stolen. When the boys found him, he'd been walking the streets for three hours and he was a quivering, starving mess. At some point, some food will be thrown at someone. A man and a woman will sit down at a table across from the boys, then promptly leave. Of all the boys, Rob's father will be the only one to notice. But the restaurant manager won't mind the noise because the boys are buying so many drinks and extra portions of egg-fried rice and chips.

'Alright then,' Rob will shout across the table, raising his glass. And it'll take Big Mike and Hucknall to quiet everyone down. 'I should have done this earlier,' Rob will shout, 'but I just wanna say thanks for all this. I know you're all wankers, but I've known you all so long —'

'So he's gonna dump Rachel and marry us!' Gareth will yell, and the boys will cheer.

'Dump the girl,' will come the shout from Larry, and Gareth will shout it too, and they'll both chant the words, banging the table. Hucknall will tell them to shut up, and Big Mike will be annoyed because that's his job, really, not Hucknall's.

Rob's father will smile and tell his son to go on with the speech.

'If I could,' Rob will say, 'I'd marry you all.'

'A toast to us!' Gareth will shout. And though his glass will be empty, he'll raise it anyway. Rob won't realise he never said what he wanted to say.

In Gogarty's, Gareth will be doing his bear-hug-picking-up-mates routine again, but the place will be packed and he'll be banging into everyone. It won't help matters that they're all dressed like potatoes. Big Mike will take Gareth aside and tell him to calm the fuck down.

Upstairs, in the smoking area, Larry and Rob – neither smoke – will be reminiscing.

'Getting older's mad, innit?' Rob will say, taking a swig of his pint. He'll almost have forgotten he's dressed like a woman, and he'll be repeatedly confused by all the looks he's getting.

'Yeah,' Larry will say. 'I can't believe we're twenty-seven. Innit sad thinking about all the things we'll never do? I was thinking about it the other day. Like, at this age, I will never be the victim of paedophilia.'

Rob will laugh and bury his head in his hands. Between his fingers, he'll see the cream foam collecting on the inside of his glass. He'll take a swig and look at Larry. 'Incredible,' he'll say.

'It's not real, though,' Larry will say. 'I reckon we're in *The Matrix*. We're gonna wake up and we're gonna be five years old and it's gonna be the end of our first day at school again and—'

'Yeah,' Rob will say.

'But back to the issue,' Larry will say. 'Any pre-match doubts?'

'What, about Rachel?'

'Yeah. Any niggles?'

'Nah, all good, mate. All good.'

'I dunno how you do it,' Larry will say – and he'll mean it now, he'll be sincere. 'My record is three weeks and four days.'

Downstairs, Rob's father will be standing on a table with a Welsh flag around his head, singing 'Don't Look Back in Anger'.

'I'm telling you,' Gareth will shout at Hucknall at the bar, 'I'm not buying a house.'

'You been with Carly five years now, though, mate.'

'I know, but I'm not buying a house.'

'Look, you bender,' Hucknall will say, 'you can't live at home all your life. I'm spending shitloads on rent in London. I know that. But at least I'm not living with my fucking parents.'

'I know,' Gareth will say, and when Hucknall turns to fetch his pint from the bar, Gareth will put his arms around Hucknall's potato waist, pick him up, and launch him into a group of French guys in the corner. Pints will be knocked over, and Hucknall will be winded. He'll get up, confused, and make apologies to the jostling French men. He'll push his way through, smile at Gareth, and gesture for him to come back. And when Gareth takes a step forward, Hucknall will smack him square in the nose. Gareth will feel the cartilage snap, the muscle tear from the bone, and he'll be buckled over when he sees Hucknall lining up another.

He'll bound for the doors then. He'll leg it out, down

the lane, down Merchant's Arch. He'll dodge and weave through the traffic, and lunge up to the bridge. He'll put his hand to his nose and there'll be blood wetting his fingers. He'll keep running until he's on the other side, on Lower Liffey Street. He'll take a seat at the bench.

He'll be sat there, watching the boardwalk, seething and lost, when a girl who's smoking outside the Grand Social will come sit beside him.

'Have a chip on your shoulder, do you?'

'What?' he'll say.

'You're a potato,' she'll say. 'Chips. Potatoes.' She'll look at him, see the nose. 'God, you're bleeding.'

'I know,' he'll say.

The taxis will be piling up beside the Liffey, glowing. Gareth will be staring at them, at the thin whistle of white lights, at the dark night, at the starless sky, at all the people on the boardwalk, and he'll think that only yesterday morning he was leaving his mother's house to get on the minibus. He'll feel small now, as if he's shrinking even, as if he's been dragged down from that vast sky and put here in Dublin, with his past and everything he knows about himself left behind. It's as if they've just brought the shell of his body over to Ireland, as if the rest of him might still be on the plane. He'll realise he hasn't looked up at the girl in some time.

'You alright?' she'll say.

He'll pause for a moment, unsure if he'll actually say it. This isn't how he imagined it. This isn't how he thought it all might go. But he'll look down at his bob-bly potato body and think *fuck it*.

'I'm gay,' he'll say, and he'll feel there's no returning now.

'Good for you,' the girl will say. 'I was just asking if you're alright.'

He'll shift over on the bench, put a hand on her shoul-der. 'No, you don't get it. My friends don't know I am. No one knows.'

'Oh God,' she'll say, watching the blood dribble from his nose, past his lips. 'I bet you're having a long night.'

'Yeah,' he'll say, getting up. 'I've got to go tell the boys.'

He'll leave the girl then, he'll rise, and he'll cross the bridge, and he'll wait at the beeping traffic lights before crossing the road. He'll wipe the blood with the sleeve of his potato costume – red streaks on the creamy-brown. He'll walk through the arch and over the cobbles to Gogarty's. The bouncers won't let him back in because he'll be too drunk, so he'll sit outside on the pavement and ring the boys. He'll call and he'll text, and Larry will come out and Gareth will go to say it, will go to tell him everything. He'll look at Larry, his fringe gelled upwards, and Gareth will open his mouth, he'll go to say how it's been like this since he was fifteen – but Larry will speak first.

'You alright?' he'll say. 'All the boys are off to find a strip club now – are you comin or what?'

There'll be a pause, a moment of nothing.

'Aye,' Gareth will finally say, 'I could probably do with seeing some tits.'

all the boys

They'll wake late on the Sunday. They'll be rushing to check out of the hostel. They won't all have breakfast together because the London boys will have an earlier flight. All the boys will hug and high-five, and the Caerphilly boys will say bye to Hucknall and Peacock as the two leave in search of a taxi.

Big Mike still won't be talking to Gareth and there'll be a tough silence in the group until Rob tells them to sort it out cos it's getting depressing. Gareth will apologise for 'ruining Gogarty's', and say he was wrecked, he doesn't remember any of last night now. He'll buy Big Mike a make-up pint and Big Mike will accept.

'Don't get me wrong,' Big Mike will say, 'Hucknall's a prick, but you don't go chucking your mates around a pub.'

Big Mike will say there's still time for them to see a little bit more of the city, but the boys won't be up for it. They've got their bags to carry, and Man Utd are on at 12.30, and can't they just watch the match at Fitzsimons? They're sure the place has Sky.

So they'll watch the United game at Fitzsimons, and they'll nurse slow pints, and they'll keep looking at their phones, sending texts to their girlfriends and wives. They'll decide to leave earlier than they need to because they're just killing time now, aren't they? There's no point waiting around here, they're better off getting to the airport than staying around here. At least they know they won't miss the flight then.

So they'll get the taxi, and they'll wait at departures, and they'll board their flight, and they'll sit there as the plane carries them over the water, over from Dublin to Bristol, and they'll wait at Bristol Airport for their minibus to pick them up, and they'll get on the minibus, and they'll tell stories about the weekend to each other, and they'll try and clear up some details that are hazy, like how much did it actually cost to get into the strip club? Did anyone else see Rob Senior on the table in Gogarty's? And Gareth, where did you get to last night, mate? What happened to you?

And when they cross the Severn Bridge, and see the *Welcome to Wales* sign, all the boys will cheer.

HOW SAD, HOW LOVELY

Down by the castle, I watched an old man sit on a bench and eat a brown-bread sandwich. He was staring off, looking at the moat. Watching him, I was brought to slow, desperate tears. Another time, seeing a small kid push his own pram through the shopping centre, I felt giddy and started weeping with tingling joy. I had to hide in the magazine aisle of WHSmith until I calmed down. But I couldn't put words to these feelings and the way they swung. Some days it felt as if the feelings weren't even inside of me. They were airborne – in Caerphilly's stupid streets – and I just happened to breathe them in.

Now the council had let me go, I was free to do what I liked. But the lack of money took inches off my height. I seemed to walk smaller, like I was afraid I might be asked to pay for the space I was taking up. And I knew that a weekly food shop was the way to save money, but I'd go into Iceland and skulk the aisles for ages, unable to think of a single meal I could make. More than once, I filled a basket to halfway before putting it down and leaving the store. But when the hunger headaches came knocking, I'd make a really sweet tea – tossing in two or three spoonfuls of sugar – then drink it slowly, willing the glucose into my blood. There were times when it felt like I was the one drowning myself, pushing on my own head as I sunk.

And I was disappointed when I found the pinworms – thin, white things curling and uncurling in my shit. And while I knew which tablets to get – I'd had worms before – I couldn't face going to the pharmacy and having that woman look at me again. So I tried to just shower every day, to wash my bedding every week. Yet I still found myself scratching at night, and having to get up to clean under my fingernails.

With no reason to wake early, I started taking lie-ins and afternoon naps. It was as if I was recovering all the sleep debt from the years I'd been working. But the lethargy soon became tiring and I fell out of the advised routines. I'd stay up till the early hours, watching detective shows until I fell asleep. When the morning light came in, I'd peel myself off the couch and climb into bed to sleep some more. Waking again at twelve or one in the afternoon, I'd lie in bed until my back ached, until I couldn't lie there any longer. Then I'd get changed into stale jeans, and head out to Glanmor's to buy a pasty, a sausage roll and a custard slice. I had just done my regular brunch trip when I ran into Emma. She was bounding out of Tesco, shopping bags looped over her arms, a wooden necklace swinging. I hadn't spoken to her since she and her boyfriend moved in next door, and I didn't want to speak to her now. It was barbecue weather, the smell of charcoaled meat wafted over garden fences, and my body lumbered as if I'd just been camping. My eyes were crusting, my shirt clung to my back, and I could feel the sweat dripping down, down all the way under the waistband of my boxer shorts. Even my arse was sweating. I didn't want to speak to anyone, but Emma stopped to talk. She actually stopped and said hello.

Her forehead was dotted with swelling acne, the kind that girls have when they're fourteen – but, as Emma would later tell me, repeatedly, she was *actually* twenty-five. She was wearing sunglasses, black and round, but I could still see her eyes peeping through the hazel lenses. The sunglasses made me uneasy. I didn't know if she could see me glaring at her spots. Walking home through the lanes, I looked straight ahead, never once looking at her. The rattle of wheels soundtracked the journey, as parents pushed empty buggies to collect their kids from the nursery.

'Aren't they creepy?' Emma whispered.

'What?' I said.

'The parents. Look how happy they are pushing those prams.'

I glanced at the mothers, their faces carved with smiles. 'You're not wrong,' I said.

When I had seen the little boy pushing his empty pram near WHSmith, it was his pride that had moved me, the dignity I imagined he felt in becoming his own master. But the parents here looked oddly smug. *Our prams might be empty now*, the smiles seemed to say, *but in a minute, we'll be important again.*

At our front doors I hesitated when Emma invited me in. Before I could say no, she had her key in the lock.

'Do you like tea?'

'Yeah,' I said.

'Good,' said Emma, and she pushed open the door. 'You can put the kettle on for us. I'm busting for the loo.'

I was struck by how cosy their place was. Standing in their living room, I imagined nestling on the couch in winter, huddled under a thick blanket, drinking a mug of mulled wine and watching films while it rained outside.

But their kitchen was in a different state. The walls were the faded pink of old plaster. And cracked tiles, the colour of smokers' teeth, rimmed the sink. Underfoot a grimy lino swelled, rucking at the edges.

As I poured the kettle, I heard the toilet flush above me, the pipes shake, then the double bounces of Emma's flip-flops down the stairs. She swished into the kitchen, retying her hair. Under the bare light, her forehead glistened with acne scars. She reached past me, opened a cupboard, and took out a plate for my pasty.

'To the living room!' she declared.

She took residence on the couch, and started talking about the local nursery – and that quickly got her talking about her mother. She told me that she had died eighteen months before – breast cancer, a long, slow death – and, additionally, that her mother had always hated Paul, Emma's boyfriend. She said that last bit with all the expectancy of someone telling a joke. But I didn't know if I should laugh.

'She was French and crazy, you see,' Emma said, coiling and uncoiling the hair at the back of her head. 'The two don't always go together but—'

'Yeah,' I said, and I tried to smile. The pose felt awkward, so I took a bite of the pasty. The corned-beef filling burned the roof of my mouth.

'Whenever I complained to her about anything, she'd just go' – and Emma put on a funny French accent for this – '"*Ah, Emma, what ees life?*" She was really weird about food too, really strict, you know? When I was little, she only ever gave me protein shakes and it messed up my stomach. I reckon that's what gave me IBS.'

'God,' I said, and the cat jumped onto the couch.

'I know,' she said, stroking it. 'What do you reckon, Lily, *what ees life?*' She twiddled Lily's fur until the cat got tired of that, and then came over to me, brushing its body against my leg. Lily felt good against my leg, not in any sexual way, just pleasant.

Emma looked at Lily and grinned. Then she stretched out her arms, like she was yawning, and began massaging her neck.

'Mind if I do some stretches?'

'Be my guest,' I said. And she got down on the carpet and did a few yoga poses. I took a bite of my pasty and watched.

I felt as if I'd been overly friendly, so I lay low and tried to avoid Emma the next while. When I left the house – for a walk, or a trip to Glanmor's or the charity shops – I'd leave via the back gate. And I tried staying indoors more, watching my detective shows, applying online for jobs, and reading the books I had picked up at Shaw Trust. But doing nothing much was tiring. I began to feel like the slugs that lay dead at my kitchen door each morning, their white trails a sad record of how little they'd achieved.

The day of my thirtieth birthday, I was woken early by the clanging of the bin men in the street. I tried to fall back asleep, but my head was heavy. I went to the living room and sat on the couch. I felt like an almost-empty kettle, when you set it to boil and you get that low, raspy sound and know you're doing damage to the metal and the coils inside. I sat on the sofa watching the news. I sat there for two hours and twelve minutes, until my bladder pressed hard. When I went to the bathroom I pissed what looked like syrup, and took gulps of water from the tap. In the kitchen I allowed myself three Rich Tea biscuits slathered with butter. Feeling my pulse return, my body refilling, a kind of self-nausea rose in me. I punched my thighs a few times.

'Get it to-fucking-gether!' I shouted, and immediately felt like an idiot.

I went online and started digging and shovelling through job sites. The agencies always advertised office-admin roles, and I would always send my CV, and I would always receive the same reply – *we've got nothing at the moment, but we'll be sure to keep your name on file.* I sometimes suspected that there were no jobs, that the websites were a government ruse to punish the unemployed. But I did find an advert for a temp job at an insurance company. And though my head felt like it was being tightened with a belt, I worked on the cover letter for forty-five minutes straight. I agonised over each word, reading and rereading the piece aloud. When it was ready to send, a Bet365 pop-up appeared. I closed the pop-up and somehow closed the email, too. I went back into my account, but the message had gone. It wasn't in my Sent Items or my Drafts. It had disappeared completely. I saw my hands go to my head, I watched them *literally* pulling at my hair.

My skin started burning up, as if my anger was boiling the blood. I opened all the windows, but I was still hot. I took a cold shower, then sat in my boxers, but I couldn't stop sweating. After a bit of investigating, I concluded that my hair was at fault, so I went to the bathroom and took a scissors and then a Bic razor to it, only stopping when I started to draw blood. And it seemed to improve things. I seemed to cool down.

But when I went to bed, I still dreamt the odd, delirious dreams you get when you're dehydrated and your brain is shrivelled. In one of the dreams, hundreds of earthworms were coming out of my bum, filling my pants. And Emma was at my front door, wanting to come in, but I could feel the pink worms crawling out, crawling down the inside of my thigh – cool and clammy against the skin. Sure enough, when I woke, there were pinworms nestling in my anus. I showered again and tried to sleep, but no sleep came.

*

There were seven charity shops in Caerphilly. From my regular visits I learned the subtle differences between them all. The one at the very top of town kept changing its name, but it always had the best clothes. The British Heart Foundation on Cardiff Road got the best DVDs, but they were twice the price of the other shops. The Shaw Trust, in the shopping centre, did a great deal on books, but you had to get there at the right time. Around 2 p.m. was when they'd restock the shelves, and I'd arrive just before, hovering around the CDs, just waiting for the woman to bring out the big box from the back room. My best haul was five Hermann Hesse paperbacks for a pound. Tenovus was also good for books, but it had a poor film range. They only put out the crap action films, with men holding guns on the covers.

I was into *Inspector Morse* at the time. I liked other detectives, too: *Miss Marple*, *A Touch of Frost,* and I was always happy to find some *Poirot*. But *Morse* was bleak and familiar. As a kid, I'd watch it with my mother as she did the Sunday-evening ironing, the sound punctuated with Mum ratcheting the thermostat, or the iron exhaling when it got thirsty. And though a lot of the *Morse* episodes were now repeated on TV, I only had the four channels and I wanted to be in charge of what I consumed. As I say, though, the British Heart Foundation was expensive but it had a good DVD range. And I was in there, flipping past VHS box sets of *Friends*, when I spotted Emma again. She was wearing a yellow vest, and I could see little red marks from where her tote bag was digging into her shoulder. She held a bundle of CDs in the crook of her arm, and she surveyed the store like a tourist. She smiled when she saw me.

'Hey,' she said. 'You cut your hair!'

'Yeah,' I said, 'I got hot.'

The radio in the shop was adjusted then. A woman's voice talking about traffic jams became staticky white noise, which became grey, and then turned into the incoming haze of 'In the Summertime'. I turned and saw the old lady behind the counter. She was reaching above her, twisting the knob on the small brown radio that sat on the shelf. I imagined a red dial on a strip of white, moving as the lady rolled through the different frequencies.

'It looks good,' Emma said, and it took me a moment to realise she meant my hair. She stepped closer then, and raised her hand to touch me. I tried not to shudder. I looked at the acne on her forehead, and imagined what it would be like to kiss her.

'Girls always say they wanna shave their head,' she said, running her hand across my scalp. 'But I'd look awful if I shaved mine. Like an alien or something.'

'You wouldn't,' I said.

'Oh, I would,' she said. Then she huffed sarcastically, and her hand fell back by her side. 'A friend of mine shaved her head once, and all my mates were like *ooh, Sophie, you look so pretty*, but she didn't. She looked like an eagle.'

I smiled, and pictured Emma sitting in my living room, sitting beside me on my couch.

'You, though,' she said, 'you wear your lack of hair very well.'

I thanked her. I went to ask about the CDs under her arm, but there was a clatter then, the noise of something collapsing. The old lady at the till had fallen. She was lying on a buckled clothes rail, blouses and coat-hangers all around her on the floor. Emma pushed her CDs onto me and rushed towards her. Two other customers hurried over too, crowded round, and Emma shouted to give the woman some air, some space. There was a hush, and then I heard high-pitched moans. They were coming from the old woman. She was clutching her left shoulder, tears running down the riverbeds of her face.

'Where does it hurt?' Emma asked, kneeling down beside her.

'It's my arm,' the woman said. 'I've broken it. They're gonna take me to hospital and I'm gonna die.'

'It's okay,' Emma told her. 'You'll be okay. My boyfriend does the X-rays.'

The radio was crackling. It was on the floor beside the old woman, not quite fully tuned in. *You got women, you got women, you got women on your mind . . .* I reached down and picked it up. The metal antenna was erect. I don't know why, but I adjusted the dial until it was tuned in.

Then Emma looked at me and I switched the radio off.

A moment later, a lady came down the stairs. She was in her forties, wearing a shirt and tie. I think she was the manager. She radiated calm.

'Are you okay, Shirley?' she asked.

'I know how it goes,' Shirley said. 'They get you in there for one thing, then they kill you with something else.'

We waited until the ambulance arrived. Shirley said her neck hurt, so the paramedics took no chances. She was put on a stretcher. As they carried her out of the shop, she was crying still.

'I don't want to be in hospital,' she said. 'I don't want to go.'

I looked at Emma. She was looping the strap of her tote bag around her finger. I remembered back to the time I was in her house, the conversations we had, and I wondered if she was thinking about her mother.

We started hanging out after that. I'd go over to hers in the afternoons, to help tile the bathroom or paint the skirting boards or whatever. They were only renting the house, but the previous tenants had been a crazy drunk couple who wrecked the place, so any decorating that didn't involve vomit or smashing windows was seen as an improvement. A couple of times, I helped Emma take carloads of broken furniture and rotting carpet to the tip in Llanbradach. She'd drive slowly, huddled over the steering wheel of her white Fiesta. I remember one time, on a dismal grey day, looking at the seagulls circling the tip, and then looking at Emma – her face scrunched with concentration as she took a corner – and I couldn't think of any other place I'd rather be.

Each afternoon, after we did our handiwork, she would play bands I'd never heard before on her CD player, and lie on the leather couch and just talk. The first time I was over after we met at the charity shop, Emma explained how she was using the time off to figure out what she wanted to do. She had a history degree, but she didn't want to teach. She wanted to do something else, she said, but she wasn't quite sure what. And Paul didn't mind, she said, so long as she did the decorating and kept the house in order.

Some mornings Emma visited Shirley at the hospital,

and in the afternoons she would tell me stories that Shirley had told her, little stories about all the famous people she'd met when she worked at the Double Diamond club in the sixties. Other times, Emma would talk about her own mother. Emma's parents had separated when she was small and her father now lived in Spain. Her mother's family had never forgiven her mother for marrying Emma's dad – or something like that – so they stopped speaking. Her mother hadn't even told them she was dying. And as Emma had no brothers or sisters, everything had fallen onto her. When the cancer was discovered, she moved back in with her mum and looked after her on her own. Well, that was until a man named Ed McCann came onto the scene. The year before she died, her mother had been chatting to Ed on the internet. They had always planned to meet, but it had never quite happened. Then, out of the blue, Emma's mum announced that Ed was coming down from Liverpool for a few days.

'You actually remind me a bit of Ed,' Emma said.

'How so?' I asked.

'It's hard to put my finger on,' she said. 'But it's something to do with me never knowing what you're thinking. Anyway –' and off she went again about Ed. Ed was a good guy, but there was something manic about him, she said. He would take her mother out shopping and they'd be gone for hours, and when Emma would call, she'd discover that Ed had driven them up to the

Brecon Beacons or Barry Island or some outdoor concert in Pontypridd.

Emma's stories often went nowhere. There'd be no punchline or moral or anything like that, but as she spoke, twirling her hair with a single finger, it just seemed like each story was a layer of snow she was pushing off a mountain. She wasn't looking to see where it fell, she just wanted it gone.

And after a few days, she did seem lighter. She didn't mess with her hair so much, and she started pontificating on all sorts of things. One day, she spent a good twenty minutes arguing that musicians should be paid by the state. Another time, she said there wasn't enough evidence to support global warming. Then one day she said that Paul liked it when she wore masks during sex.

'What kind of masks?' I said.

'Celebrities,' she answered. 'Actors, mainly.'

I asked her where they got the masks from, but she looked at me and laughed.

She was very generous during all this. She gave me little presents: books, DVDs, and even a mix CD that she made especially. (She titled it 'Music School Dropout'. I still listen to it sometimes.) And they were bliss, really, those hours I sat there, and Emma lay all casual, her tanned neck gracefully moving as her head bobbed to whatever music we were listening to. Those afternoons felt like the last throes of a sickness, when you're over the worst, but you take one more day off work, and the stolen freedom feels glorious.

And I actually got offered a job. An agency called and said: just turn up 9 a.m. Wednesday and it's yours, but I couldn't make my mind up. Paul worked and it meant he never got to see Emma. I just didn't understand why anyone would want a job. Money aside, the work thing made no sense to me. On the Tuesday before the Wednesday, I sat down and finally opened my bank statements. It was bad, but not quite as bad as I had feared. I worked out that if I did proper food shops and stopped buying crap, I could last another month or maybe six weeks – enough to see through the summer at least. I decided to sleep on it, to wake early and take it from there.

I woke at noon the next day. *So,* I thought, *that's that decided, then.* I had no regrets, but that afternoon I noticed I was biting my nails a lot. I was rubbing my nose, too. And chewing on my fingers. This used to happen when work got stressful, but the thing was, I actually felt alright now. But my hands didn't agree. It was as if they were uncomfortable being a part of me. I realised the biting and chewing wasn't hygienic, especially with the worms, so I devised ways to keep my hands occupied. Walking past the nursery, I clicked my fingers. As I crossed the bridge over the moat, I clapped and tapped rhythms on myself. Strolling past the ducks, I put my hands on my head, like I was made to in school, when I'd been naughty and sent to the headmaster. And

I didn't recognise my shadow now the hair had gone. I looked oddly sharp and efficient. It felt good, though. It felt like I was regaining control of something.

It was too hot to keep walking. When I reached Morgan Jones Park I sat in the shade of a tree opposite the tennis courts. There were two guys playing, with their fat friend acting as umpire. He was standing beside the net, stuffing his face with crisps. And the guys didn't look like tennis players. One of them had his top off, which seemed a bit aggressive. He had this green snake tattoo, which started on his back and coiled over his shoulder, down to his chest. Between points, he was shouting about cars and some guy called Robbie who was getting out of prison the following week. When the park warden came round to collect money, the guy got angry and insisted that someone had already been. The fat friend took his wallet out from his pocket, but the guy told the warden he'd ALREADY paid for the FUCKING court.

So I settled on a different bench, again in the shade, near the kids' splash pad. There was a little black boy running topless through the spray, and a girl in a white dress who ran away from the fountain every time it shot out a jet. They were both six or seven, and the way the girl looked at the boy it was clear she spent her days thinking about him. But she was scared of running through that jet of water. She was agonising over it, looking fretfully over her shoulder as the boy crept up to push her in. Her little legs were moving on the spot.

And when she did take steps forward, she'd change her mind and then quickly step back. It was as if she was weighing up the gains and the losses of love. How sad, I thought. But also, how lovely.

I kept wanting to bite my nails, so I put my hands together, interlocked the fingers and pushed them away. They came back to me though, so I pulled at each finger until they clicked. Then I sat on my hands to keep them still. But watching the boy, the water shining off his dark skin, and hearing the girl finally giggle as she got soaked in the fountain's spray – the laugh echoing through the park – a surge of something filled me from the inside; it rose until my hairs stood on end and my skin was goose-pimpled. I felt myself smiling, watching them both, but also overawed, like I was at the verge of some breakthrough. I watched the leaves of the trees tremor in a light breeze and I was suddenly content. I thought if I could hold onto this feeling, if I could stretch the moment, like a skin over the rest of my life, I wouldn't need anything. I didn't need a job. The ways and means of a good life rested inside all of us.

I suddenly felt a little guilty for having judged the topless guy playing tennis. He was entitled to take off his shirt. It was hot, and he was running around, and he was just expressing his own freedom. Like the boy running in and out the water! I was thinking this and staring at nothing when a stocky bloke, around my age, approached. The bloke came right up to me and said, what are you doing? I tried to explain, but I was stuttering a lot, which seems to happen when I'm in a good mood. Behind the bloke, the kids had stopped running. They were standing there and watching us. I'm just enjoying the day, I said. The bloke looked at me. Yeah? he said. Yeah, I said, feel the breeze through the trees! Well, I think you're fucking sick in the head, the bloke said, and if you don't get the fuck out of here, I'll break your fucking face. And though I knew I was in trouble, I wasn't afraid. I just felt an odd and bountiful love for the man. I wanted to hug him, and I wanted to hug the guys playing tennis. And the park warden, and the boy running through the water, and the girl edging back, and also that old man weeks ago who ate the sandwich in the park and made me cry. Even when the bloke head-butted me, I felt at ease and untethered. As I ran out of the park, my legs burning, it was elation I felt, not fear. When the woman at the chip shop saw the blood and asked if I was okay, I said yes, yes, I'm fine, and I ordered battered sausage and chips, and funnelled all my change into the tip jar.

At home, I showered again, and put on the only clean shirt I could find. It started raining, full sheets teaming down, smacking the cars and bouncing off the pavement. So I opened the living-room window and poked my head out, watching the street pulsate. The black-tiled roofs of the houses were shining wet, and puddles were emerging in the potholes and dips of the road. In their pools, I saw the reflections of the grey-white sky. And on my cheeks I felt the breeze that comes with summer rain. It felt so lovely I clambered out the window and went next door.

It was obvious Emma had been crying when she let me in. Her eyes were red and the blood vessels pinked the whites. I asked what the matter was, but she just ran her hands through her hair and tugged at her ponytail. I sat her down on the couch and made us tea. When I came back in, she had her head in her hands. I rested her cup on the carpet.

'Do you want to talk about it?' I asked, sitting beside her.

'I was at the hospital earlier,' she said quietly.

'Okay,' I said.

'Shirley's kidneys are going.' And then she crumpled. She leaned over and hugged me, crying into my side. I sat there for a few minutes, as she lay curled on the couch, with her head in my lap. I stroked her hair until her breathing calmed. It was agony, having her head resting there. I could feel the tingle of blood flowing to my dick, pushing against my trousers, and I was worried she'd feel it against her cheek. So I tried putting the thought out of my mind. I looked around the room instead.

'Does Shirley know?' I said. Emma didn't answer.

The curtains were drawn, but the window was open, and I could see the rain coming it, soaking the top of the blue material. When I glanced down again, I noticed

Emma had a small bald patch on the crown of her head. It was red and sore-looking. There were small hairs, like stubble, and the skin around it was flaking. I considered the bald patch and thought about kissing it. A little kiss, an affectionate one to show I cared. I dipped my chin, but at the last moment she looked up and kissed me on the lips.

'Are you sure?' I said.

'You taste like salt,' she said.

She kissed me again, then sat up. She crossed her arms and brought her hands to her T-shirt, and started lifting it – the way girls do – until it was over her head. Her skin was brown and her bra was pink. She tossed the T-shirt on the floor, and climbed on top of me.

'Look,' I said.

'Don't talk,' she said, and she moved her lips to mine again.

I stroked her back and she ran her hand over my head, tracing the shape of my skull. Her skin was lovely, not a spot of acne on her body. She kissed my neck, then whispered, 'Do you want me to wear a mask?'

There was a moment. Her breathing tickled my ear, then I told her no.

She sighed and gave a childish pout. 'Please,' she said.

She left for the bedroom. I could hear her shuffling through drawers, and the rain scattering at the windows, and a pulse beating firmly in my ear. When she came back, she was naked except for a pair of black knickers.

And she was wearing a Natalie Portman mask.

'Hi,' she said.

'I haven't got—'

'Don't worry,' she said, and she reached down and slowly removed her knickers.

I was already hard by the time she came over, so she climbed on top of me and pushed me inside her. I could see her eyes moving through the peepholes, and all the while I was torn between wanting to look at her and needing to look away. I was afraid it'd be over too soon if I watched her arched neck or listened too intently. And I was afraid to change position in case she touched my bum, in case the worms were out and wriggling. But none of that happened. I held her firmly and she grinded against me, with Natalie Portman for a face. And all the while, the cat looked on from the carpet. When we finished, we lay on the couch – my head on her chest – and she stroked my scalp. We even fell asleep. When we woke, all she said was:

'Do you want a cuppa tea?'

After I left, I went to the pharmacist on Cardiff Road and bought a box of Vermox. The woman at the till didn't even bother looking at it. She just scanned the box and put it in a plastic bag.

I felt a small charge in me the rest of the evening, like something was rattling in my blood. My self felt like a stirring song, the moment when it surges, and builds, and the drums are going mad, and the guitars are whirring, and everything is at the crest of something else. I did press-ups and sit-ups, watching my body tighten and contract in my wardrobe mirror. I hoovered my bedroom. I scrubbed the shower clean, and I did the washing-up. I was exhausted, and in bed by eleven, but I couldn't sleep. I kept thinking of things to say to Emma, and I'd write them down, turn the light off, put my head on the pillow, and then another sentence would rise up again. I'm not even sure I slept that night.

The next day, I called over earlier than usual. When she switched on the kettle, I brushed her hair behind her ear, and kissed her on the neck. But her shoulders flinched.

'No offence,' she said, pulling away, 'but yesterday just didn't feel right.'

I stood there, not a single word in my head.

'It's nothing against you,' she said. 'You know how sometimes it isn't there?'

'How do you mean?' I said.

'You know,' she said, her hand going to her hair, 'when it's just not there between two people, the connection or whatever you wanna call it.'

'Oh.'

'You okay?' she said.

'Yeah.'

'You sure it's okay?'

'Yeah,' I said. 'I understand.'

'That's good,' she said, and the kettle clicked off. 'I knew you'd think the same.'

We drank tea in the living room. I don't remember much of what we spoke about, other than the news about Shirley.

'The hospital got it wrong,' Emma explained. 'Her kidneys are fine. All going well, she'll be out in a few days.'

'That's really great,' I said, and my stomach dropped to my legs.

That evening, I moved my bed against the wall, to be closer to Emma. I could hear her and Paul having sex, so I put a cup to the wall and listened. I wanked off there and then, eventually spurting onto my sheets. But in the nights after, when I heard their sounds, I'd just be tormented. I'd slam my bedroom door, or I'd punch the bed, or I'd run downstairs and sleep on the couch.

We still saw each other, but after the decorating was finished she began to look for work. And the more she got into the idea of finding a job, the more she started getting onto me about my own stuff. One day, over at her place, she was at me again, nagging, telling me to get a grip, to sort my life out.

'You are not my mother,' I shouted at her, 'and you know what, you're not my fucking girlfriend either.'

She cried. She told me I reminded her of her father. She said I listened, but I never gave. I never shared. She said I acted calm, but underneath I was probably a psycho. She said I had unresolved anger issues. She told me to get out of her house. I went back to my place and punched the couch until my arms ached. Then I went to the Wheatsheaf and spent two weeks' food budget in one shitty night. I bought drinks for people I'd never met, and played pool with a group of teenagers I knew were laughing at me whenever I turned my back. The evening ended with me vomiting my £6 seekh kebab into the corner of the Tourist Information car park.

The next day I left the house through the back gate. I turned my phone off and went to Tesco. I bought six litres of milk, two loaves of white bread, a box of fish fingers, a box of white wine, and ten packs of 14p noodles. I stayed indoors for a week. I stopped washing my clothes. And flies gathered round the rubbish bag I couldn't face putting out. I was a montage of bad living. Until the very end of August, that is, when I found the pile of Hermann Hesse books I'd bought at Shaw Trust. I started with *Siddhartha* and read it in one sitting. I read *Peter Camenzind* the next day, then *Knulp* and *Wandering* the day after. I finished off with *Klingsor's Last Summer,* and I felt unreal. Literally unreal, as if I wasn't in my body any more. A notch, a dial, had rotated inside me, like on a safe. I was changed. For years, I had thought of myself as a kettle, with a little red bobbing gauge. And now I was filled again – the gauge was at my chest, and rising, rising, on the verge of flight.

We shouldn't work, Hesse was telling me. Responsibilities enslave us. We have to commit our lives to finding meaning. And even if I didn't go along with everything he thought about adventures and solitude, the message was clear: we had to fight if we wanted to be free.

I spent the evening writing lyrics and poems for Emma, but none of them captured what I wanted to say. In the end, I made her a mix CD. And instead of a track listing, I wrote out a corresponding memory to each song: *the time we tiled the bathroom; the time you cheated at Monopoly; the time you made me laugh so hard I almost peed.* And in between those memories, I copied out lines from Hesse, lines I knew she needed to read.

The next morning, when I knocked at Emma's door, I couldn't tell if she was glad to see me. But all the same, she invited me in. On the living-room floor, she had a Scrabble board set up. She sat down beside it, arranging the tiles on the carpet.

'I'm sorry,' I said. 'I've been a mess, I know. I'm still a mess, but I feel so much better now.'

She nodded and tapped a Scrabble piece on the carpet floor. 'It's fine,' she said, and she went to say more but then said nothing. I stood there, not knowing where to look. There were plates and magazines strewn across the couch. Clothes spilled out of a red basket on the tea table, and one of the curtains was half-detached from its rail.

'Can I sit down with you?'

'Free world,' she said.

I wanted to tell her everything. How Hesse had written

about the things we had spoken about; how the stories had saved me; made me both calmer and full-blooded, and how I was ready for anything. But it didn't seem right now. And the feelings began to mutate while I was in the room. They didn't seem firm or graspable, or something I could even explain.

We sat there in silence, and when it got too much, I realised I'd been hasty. I apologised and gave her the CD.

'Look,' she said, and she put the CD on the carpet. She didn't even look at it. 'This isn't about you. Honest, I'm glad you're here. I forgave you ages ago, anyway.'

'Really?'

Emma gripped a Scrabble piece, and I thought of how she had gripped her tote bag in the British Heart Foundation.

'Wait,' I said, 'is it Shirley?'

'She's fine,' Emma said, and she pushed the Scrabble piece around the palm of her hand. 'It's just me. I think I might be a little bit pregnant.'

I thought of my sperm rushing inside her, of how we clutched each other.

'When did you—?'

'I'm not going to keep it,' she said. 'And before you ask: no, it'd be his.'

*

They named her Natalie. Emma thought the house was too small for the baby, so they moved to a semi in Castle View. It's odd, but even though this all happened a few years back, I keep thinking about that living room and the couch. Is the couch still there, I wonder? Did they take it to the new house? Does she ever sit on it and think of me?

The last time I saw her was Bonfire Night just gone. I was wandering down by the castle, and there she suddenly was, beside the doughnut van, with little Natalie up on her back. The two of them were wrapped in scarves, hats and gloves. Emma's hair was short under her beanie, and her skin looked much better. I pretended I hadn't seen her, but when I snuck one more look she saw me and waved me over.

'Well,' she said, 'how the hell are you? How are you spending your time these days?'

I appreciated the question's phrasing, its lack of the words 'work' or 'job'. But when I told her about my night work at the call centre, she lifted Natalie down and said she was really glad I was doing well.

I could smell the cinnamon from the doughnut van, almost taste the dough. A man over the tannoy system spoke about fire safety and sparklers. Little Natalie gripped Emma's hand then buried her face in her lap, and Emma explained how Natalie had only just started nursery and hated it so much that she would make up all sorts of elaborate excuses not to go. 'She's a nutter,'

Emma said. Then she said she might be a bit mad herself, because she was finally considering doing teacher's training. I told her she'd make a great teacher, and she smiled, a genuine smile.

Paul waddled up then, carrying two steaming cups of tea with a paper bag of doughnuts resting on top. 'How's it going?' he said, and without a word, Emma took the doughnuts off him – and he placed a cup of tea in her empty hand. It was a simple act, but the intimate choreography filled me with quiet awe.

When the booming and the screeching started, Natalie put her hands over her ears and we all cast our eyes to the heavens. Streaks of light scorched above the castle then, as fireworks lit white rips in the deep, black sky. All of us together watched for a dizzying while, then they left, and I watched them walk away.

In fairness to Emma, whenever we run in to each other, she'll always stop for a chat. But the conversation is different now. It never really feels solid – it's like we're heaping snow on top of more snow, on top of a shaky mountain. Our words are light in case of avalanche.

And I know what it's like when it all comes down. Things were heavy for a long while, but I'm hopefully through the worst. I've started seeing a girl who works at the call centre, and it's going well, I think. She's kind, and she seems to understand me. We're taking it steady, though. She has her own issues, her own set of problems – and the truth is, there are times when I can't bear to be in this skin of mine, times when I get so low that the smallest demands seem impossible.

And every few months the worms come back. Apparently they lay their eggs at night.

NOS DA

After the kids have gone to school, he watches his wife climb into bed. He turns up the volume and presses his palms against his headphones, as if to squeeze Karen's sounds deeper into his ears. He watches for five, ten, fifteen minutes, until she is asleep.

He changes the channel and watches Aled. Aled is sitting at his classroom table, practising handwriting, his little tongue poking out the side. Karen does it when she's concentrating too, and Richard wonders where in the DNA is the code for that?

A kid steals Aled's ruler, and Richard watches as Aled swings a slap across his face. He watches as the boy reddens with tears and the teacher marches over and speaks in firm tones. He watches as Aled offers a hand and says sorry, that it was just an accident.

Karen is awake now, and Richard watches as she stands on the landing and separates a bundle of laundry into darks and whites. He watches as she rinses the breakfast bowls and casts them upside down on the drying rack.

His pocket vibrates: a text from Lisa.

'*I'm sorry about last night. I shouldn't have got upset. I'll make it up to you tonight. Fancy something nice for dinner? xxx*'

Onscreen, Karen is bending down and hoovering beneath the couch.

'*It's okay*,' he replies to Lisa. '*Yeah, something nice would be nice indeed.*'

When he switches to his daughter's channel, she is standing in the queue at the school canteen. She chooses her dinner – a pizza slice and a side of chips – then carefully carries her plate to a table in the corner of the hall. He watches as she sits on her own, tangling her ponytail as she slowly chews a chip. The girls at her table whisper to one another, and Richard wants to reach in, reach into the screen and hug her.

His ears are beginning to burn and ache from the headphones. He removes them, places them on his lap, and changes the channel back to his wife. Soundlessly, he watches as Karen steps into the car on the driveway, as she starts the engine, as she belts up. And he watches as she turns off the ignition, unbelts, gets out of the car, and checks that the front door is locked. She's always been anxious, but she's definitely been worse these last few months.

He can hear noises from the other booths in the corridor now. The wails and the laughter and the hum of chatter: the talking and the pleading with the people onscreen.

'*See you later xxx*' the text from Lisa says, and already he is late for work.

He works in the same building that his mother used to bring him to for Sunday School. But the chapel is now a series of offices and the walls are painted white and the floors are carpeted grey with eighties-style red stripes. The corridors smell, he thinks, like mashed potato. He's been doing the job for three weeks, but it doesn't feel like it's getting any easier.

Today, he is working on a Combined Film for a man called Bryn and his wife Sue. The application was sent in the day he arrived, and since then the interns downstairs have been collecting the memory files together. In his cramped office, Richard takes the raw days, then cuts and edits them into scenes. For some of the memories, Bryn has requested particular songs. Richard follows the guidelines, but he still makes mistakes. When he exports an early chapter he accidentally chooses the wrong colour settings, and Bryn's childhood scene at Porthcawl beach suddenly looks like a bluey negative. He messes up the soundtrack exports, too, and 'Knockin' on Heaven's Door' is put on loop throughout the film. It adds a beautiful poignancy to the scene of Bryn and Sue's wedding, but it's not really the desired effect.

He's only part-time for now, but he's been told there's a good chance he'll be made full-time in the run up to

Christmas. And he could do with the money. The Full Package subscription for the Viewing Booths is beyond his wage, and he's not sure how much longer he can tolerate the adverts and the usage limits. Sometimes, when he should be working, he tots up his finances on a piece of paper and tries to think of ways of cutting back, of making and saving money.

Onscreen it's 1984, and Sue and Bryn and their kids are in pedalos on Roath Park Lake. The daughter is in with Bryn, and the son is in with Sue, and they are racing across the lake, and the daughter is screaming, 'Faster, Daddy!', and the sun is shining off the ripples and every-one is beaming.

Richard is meant to be out by six, but it's 5.30 and he's done nowhere near enough work on the film. He texts Lisa to say he'll be home late. On the computer, he launches Sue's Memory Directory: thousands of folders and files, all tagged and named by the interns down-stairs. Sue has requested that he doesn't use any material from 1981–1983. On the application form she says she was unwell during those two years, and she wouldn't be able to bear looking at how she was. Richard scrolls through, marking up the requisite folders. He hasn't eaten since breakfast and his ears throb with hunger.

By 7 p.m. he has somehow lost a chapter, so he spends an hour on the computer trawling the folders and files to find the right memory. He's searching through the *1980 > Genesis* folder, when he hears footsteps outside the editing suite. He feels himself straighten. Then a man with a grey moustache enters, shining a torch into Richard's face.

'It's half eight,' the guard says. 'No one's meant to be here after seven.'

Richard's monitor is crammed with a full-screen image of Sue and Bryn. In the footage, they're in their early forties, standing by a fence in a field at night. There are other people nearby, mostly girls and women, holding banners and wearing Phil Collins T-shirts.

'I'm sorry,' Richard says. 'I didn't know.'

The man gestures at the monitor. 'That's a big screen, that is,' he says. 'What you watching anyway?'

'It's a Memory Tape,' Richard says.

'Good God,' the man says. 'You make them here? In this tiny place?'

Richard nods.

'I've actually been thinking about getting one done,' the man says. 'Expensive, mind, ain't they?'

The security guard sits himself down. He's a big man, with massive hands. He has stocky legs, which bulge through his trousers. He tells Richard he used to be a sports teacher in St Martin's, and Richard sees there might once have been definition to the man's bulk.

'Yeah, I was there for ten years, and then one day we were coming back from a competition in Brecon,' the man says. 'The boys had just won the Welsh Championships. It was tight but they won the relay and that sealed it. Anyway, we were all singing songs on the way home, and the boys were getting a bit rowdy, nothing too bad – but I could tell that things were on the cusp of getting silly, you know? I was driving the minibus, I was, and I turned around to tell them to calm down, and I didn't see the corner.'

Richard smiles, and then realises that he shouldn't really be smiling, so he bobs his head and drops the smile as he nods.

'But I wouldn't want the crash to be in my film,' the man says. 'You know what I mean? I lived through it once, I don't need to see it again. Anyway' – and he points at the screen – 'what happens next?'

Richard clicks play, and the scene unfolds: Phil Collins leans over the railing and kisses Sue on the cheek.

'Ah, isn't that amazing?' the man says. 'God, I wonder what I'd choose to have in mine.'

Lisa's watching a film on the TV when he gets back. She is sloped on the couch, drinking wine and smoking a cigarette.

'So sorry I'm late,' he says. 'How's it going?'

Her mouth is smiling, but her eyes are doing something else, as if to say: *what a stupid question*.

'Work was crazy,' he says, and he sits at the table. He folds one leg over the other, and pulls off his shoe. 'How was the cafe?'

'Top drawer,' she answers, and he can feel her eyeing

him over, working out his story. 'Yeah,' she says, 'no one can put a sandwich on a plate as good as me.' She runs her hand through her red hair and takes out the black bobble. She puts it over her wrist and shakes her hair down.

'How were they then?' she says.

'Who?'

'You're two hours late,' she says. 'Don't tell me you were in work till now.'

'I texted you,' he says, pulling off the other shoe. 'I was in work.'

'Until nine?' she says, and she turns the volume down on the film. 'You're meant to be part-time.'

'I know,' he says. 'It's called trying to make a good impression.'

'Well, I can't remember the last time you tried that with me.' There's a pause, a moment of nothing, and Richard thinks this could go either way. 'Anyway, she says. 'How are they? Has Aled calmed down yet?'

'He's still angry,' Richard says. 'And Rhian's still quiet.'

'And what about your wife? How is *she* today?'

'I didn't watch her,' he says.

'No?'

'No,' he says, and he feels his voice break more than it should. 'And anyway, we're so busy at work. I only really watched for a little bit this morning.'

She looks back at the TV and nods.

'Speaking of work,' she says, 'I'm away this weekend. We're doing catering for a wedding.'

'Another one?' he says, and he thinks again about how much she's worked recently, and how different she's been this last while. Last night, before the argument, she'd been looking at her phone throughout dinner and it had really pissed him off. But he wonders now if something else is going on. Maybe she's seeing someone else, he thinks, and the thought doesn't upset him as much as it should. With Karen, he would sometimes try to imagine her with another man, but he couldn't get upset about it. He'd get hypothetically competitive, but not jealous. Does that mean it wasn't love?

'Your dinner's in the oven,' she says. 'And I got you the ice cream you like. It's in the freezer.'

'Thanks so much,' he says, and he knows that he sounds like a person trying to rush amends.

'No bother,' she says, not looking up from the telly.

When they get to bed, Lisa's still wearing the top she wore in the day. Richard wonders if it's some kind of passive-aggressive gesture. In case he's reading it wrong, he cwtches up to her and strokes her breasts through the top. She slowly shifts. Then he strokes her neck and kisses her, but she sits up.

'Is this how it's gonna be all the time?' she says.

'What you mean?'

'You going there and leaving me here.'

'I was *in work*,' he says. 'I told you.' He sits up and reaches for a glass of water on the bedside table. The glass feels cool in his hand.

'You're not the same after you've been,' she says. 'It takes you ages to come back.'

'Oh come on,' he says, and he wants to say: just leave it, please, not now. He sips the water and it tastes slightly off, almost dusty. An old fact he once read comes unbidden: that the molecules in water are billions of years old. He thinks now of all the stomachs and rivers and drains this water has passed through; all the pipes it climbed to come up the tap then down into his glass.

'No,' she says. 'No "come on". I felt bad about last night, so I went out and bought you all the food you like, all the things you like. And then you don't come back till hours after cos you're at the bloody Viewing Booths.'

Her eyes look tired. They're bloodshot and strained. He can feel a dull ache in his stomach and he suspects it's because of the dusty water. 'I wasn't there,' he says. 'And even if I was—' he breaks off.

'What?' she says.

'Look,' he says, 'you've got no idea what it's like to lose your kids.'

She sighs, and the sigh sounds performative to him. 'No, I *don't*,' she says. 'But I've been here a lot longer than you, and I know you've got to fucking let go. You can't be in two places at once.'

He goes to speak, but she turns off the light and says *nos da* – it's Welsh for 'good night', but tonight she means it as another way of saying, *no more*. *Nos da*, he replies and he takes another sip of the water. In the darkness he returns the glass to the bedside table, and he feels a small sense of pride for performing the task so ably. But the moment quickly passes, and five minutes later, he is sinking into sleep, and he is almost wistful about it. He's never had problems sleeping, but he knows that she sees it as uncaring. He should be tossing and stirring, and waking up tomorrow, sounding contrite ('I didn't sleep a wink') – but that's not how his body works. If he's overwhelmed, he sleeps.

*

Lisa's still asleep when Richard leaves, and he is up and out early. He buys a croissant and a coffee from Tesco and heads to the Viewing Booths at the top of town. The queues are long in the morning, but they move quickly. Once he's through security he hurries to the lift and finds an empty booth. Onscreen, his kids sit at the kitchen table with their cornflakes, and Karen stands by the radiator, her hands holding its rim.

'We've got ten minutes,' she says. 'No delays, alright?'

And with that, Aled promptly spills his apple juice. Karen looks like she's about to shout, but Aled laughs and goes, 'I look like I've done a mega wee *all over* my trousers.' And Karen laughs, and Rhian laughs, and Richard takes a sip of his coffee and smiles.

He watches them brush their teeth. He watches them move through the house. He watches them run from the door to the car, coats held over their heads to shield them from the rain.

Karen sits in the passenger seat and turns on the ignition. The wipers swipe left, then swipe right, and she stares at the house for a moment.

'You locked it,' Rhian says. 'I saw you.'

'I did, didn't I?' Karen says, and she slaps her thighs, then reverses the car out of the drive.

The bus feels oddly quiet. Sitting beside Richard is a young guy with a beard. He is wearing white earplugs, and on his phone he is watching another young man drive a car. Behind Richard, two older women are on their phones. He can't see what they're watching, but their eyes are locked on the screen. Every now and then they swipe right, then swipe left. He thinks: when I've saved up enough, I'll definitely get the app.

At work, there are three voice messages from Sue, the woman whose film he's working on. *Please call me back*, she says, *please*.

When he calls, her voice is almost a whisper. 'It's not easy to talk about,' she says. 'Can I come into the office?'

He tells her they're really busy, but she pleads. When she arrives an hour later, he takes her through to the small meeting room, where blue boxes of video tapes line the shelves.

Sue is seventy-six – he knows this from the forms – but she seems younger. She is small, her hair is silver, but she is far from frail. She's holding a set of car keys, and as she speaks, she runs her finger along the serrated edges.

'Bryn,' she says, 'he was the one who wanted the film made. And I know I signed off on the permissions, but, you see . . . well, look . . . it happened a long time ago, and it was so stupid. He'd been working a lot of hours, you know. I never saw him.'

'Okay,' Richard says.

'This was when the kids were little, you know? And it only happened once. And I felt awful. But it was just one of those things. And I spent my whole life worried about him finding out. And when he died, a tiny part of me – and you're going to think I'm awful for saying this – but, well, a tiny, tiny part of me felt relieved cos it meant he'd never find out.' She pauses and kneads her hands.

'It's alright,' Richard says. 'Nothing will go in that you don't want to go in.'

'But have you seen it?' she says. 'Who else has seen it? How many people know?'

He explains the process, how it's mostly done with computers, and how the interns are only there to label and tag the big stuff. But all the while, he's thinking about the times he cheated on Karen. He never really felt bad about it. After the first time, he took a bath and he thought there'd be something purifying about the act – cleansing – but as he lay there, he found himself pissing, the water between his legs clouding yellow.

'I haven't been here long,' he says to Sue, 'but trust me, we get far, far worse.'

Sue rubs at her wedding ring, massages the knuckle. 'I just dunno what I'd do if he ever found out,' she says. 'He's the kindest man I've ever known.'

When Sue leaves, Richard sends Lisa a text: *'Let me take you out tonight.'*

*

She's doing the dishes, so she doesn't see him come into the cafe. He watches her from behind. She's in full uniform – tuxedo and a fez, her hair not even reaching her shoulders – and it strikes him as odd, now, that her shape is something so familiar. He could pick out the back of her, or even a fragment of her voice, from a line-up of a thousand. But still he can't give himself fully to her. Why, he wonders, is he designed so poorly?

Lisa still hasn't seen him. She is looking at her phone, and her shoulders are shaking as if she's laughing.

'Well,' she says, when she eventually turns and sees him. 'Of all the Tommy Cooper-themed cafes, in all the towns, and you walk into mine.'

'There are others?' he says.

'Well, no, but you know what I mean.' She is chewing some gum and her smile is warm, and he knows this evening will be okay.

She makes him coffee, and he sits by the window waiting for her shift to finish. It's dark out, and as the traffic ambles down Cardiff Road he thinks of the arguments he and Karen had over the years. There were times when he was too stubborn, and times he was too selfish when he should have compromised.

Lisa comes over and kisses him on the cheek. She's wearing a denim jacket and she looks like she's ready to start the evening, her whole life, everything, afresh. But maybe that's just him, he thinks. He often swings between these two poles: either he is completely alone in the world and no one knows a thing about him, or he believes that everyone is thinking the same as him, that everyone is in a similar emotional place.

'What were you laughing at earlier?' he says.

'You what?' she says, and she looks at her reflection in the window and adjusts her fringe.

'On your phone,' he says.

'Oh that,' she says. 'It was just a video. I'll show it to you later.'

On the screen above the door, Tommy Cooper plays the trumpet and laughs.

They go to the cinema and they go for food. Afterwards they walk hand in hand through Caerphilly, and there's a lightness to their stride. He feels it in his chest. It's like the opposite of anxiety, and it spreads through him like that August evening he spent wandering through a village in France when he was twenty-one.

Near the Boar's Head, a deathday party swings its way up the street. A group of women in cowboy hats and devil horns are laughing and leading the deathday woman into the pub. She's in torn clothes, with fake blood smeared over her face. She's swaying on her heels, and she leans a moment against the wall. She remains still long enough for Richard to get a look at the white T-shirt she's wearing. Her face is printed on the back. Beneath the photo it says in a green, ghoully font: 'Dead Ten Years And Never Felt Better!'

Caerphilly Castle is lit orange tonight. The light shimmers in the moat, and Richard thinks that if he were a child now, he'd believe the orange glow on the castle was coming from the water itself. In the black sky, he sees pinpricks of white light and the longer he looks, the more he sees: hundreds and hundreds of stars. For all he knows, they mightn't even be real, but either way, he thinks, there's a life here to be lived.

At the roundabout, he sees Sue and Bryn on the grass, walking a tortoise on a lead. Richard waves, and Bryn calls out, 'How you doin?'

'Good,' Richard shouts back. 'You?'

Bryn gestures at the tortoise, and then all around him. 'It's just so hard to find a good patch of grass.'

And to show he's listening, Richard looks around and stares at the high-rise flats that stand above Caerphilly, like massive audio speakers set on mute. 'You're not wrong,' he calls back, and Bryn smiles and waves, and Sue waves too.

Richard and Lisa keep walking, then, laughing, and saying Bryn's line to each other in funny voices. They pass the shopping centre and the quiet, grey-haired man who always sits with a picture of Jesus beside him. Tonight he holds a handmade yellow banner that says in big letters: '*He that overcometh shall not be hurt of the second death*'. And for a moment, Richard feels nostalgic for the faith he had as a child, for the world conjured by the coloured drawings in the Children's Bible his mother had given him. And that good feeling moves in him and becomes something he feels towards Lisa.

When they're down by the chip shop at the Pic, he puts a hand on her shoulder and says, 'Wait, I've got something for you.' He dips his other hand deep into his pocket and rummages. 'Okay,' he says. 'I've got it. You hafta close your eyes, though.'

Lisa duly obliges, and Richard places his hands on her cheeks, and gives her a deep, deep kiss. He can feel her lips smiling.

'What was that for?' she says.

'Ah, I'm just sorry,' he says. 'I know I've been a prick.'

'No, no,' she says, her hands suddenly animated. 'I'm

the one who's been a pain. I mean, of course you'd want to see her.' She runs her hands through her hair then. 'Actually, I've got you a present. A real one, though. Cos I'm not a tight-arse like you.'

She reaches into her bag, and takes out a silver envelope. She passes it to him, and he opens it slowly. Inside he finds two tickets. 'Tommy Cooper?' he says, and his voice is high with excitement.

'Yeah!' she says. 'He's coming in a few weeks. Crazy, isn't it?'

'That's mad,' he says. 'Thank you thank you thank you.'

'My pleasure,' she says, and she takes the tickets back before he can lose them.

'You are right though,' he says. 'About the Viewing Booths, I mean. They're not—'

'The problem's me, not you,' she says. 'Anyway, I've worked it all out now. I've got attachment and abandonment issues.'

'You what?'

'I was googling it earlier,' she says. 'I'm scared of people leaving unexpectedly. It's cos of the way I died.'

*

The weather gets colder and his bones ache with it. The mornings are especially hard, but Lisa has started doing early shifts at the cafe, and she makes Richard get up with her in the dark crawl of day.

'It's just nice to have breakfast with someone,' she says. 'It's good for the health.'

So for the first time in either life he starts getting out of bed as soon as the alarm goes off. No snoozing, no turning over.

He begins to lose count of how many films he has made. And it seems unfathomable to him – when he first started the job it took a week to make just one. But he's pumping them out. Since he went full-time, things have come together. And yes, he's been doing more hours than he'd like, but he is making and saving money, and that's what's important.

And things are improving with Lisa. Now he's working more and spending less time at the Booths, they're getting somewhere, they're moving forward.

He's still going to the Booths, of course – and he goes more often than he tells Lisa – but it is hard to find the time. And anyway, the more hours he works – and the more money he saves – the sooner he can subscribe to the Full Package.

*

He remembers the first time he saw Tommy Cooper on the TV. Richard was only young and his father was lying on the couch, almost crying with laughter as Tommy Cooper did the hat trick.

'Born in Caerphilly!' his father proudly told him, and

his mother, sitting on the other chair, replied straight away: 'Yeah, but he left when he was four and never came back.' But still, that was enough for Richard – he was astonished that someone from his town could be there on screen.

And he is thinking of his parents now; he is thinking of them as there's a knock at the door and Bryn and Sue enter the editing suite.

'I just wanted to shake your hand,' Bryn says, and he does just that. Richard sits them down and fills the kettle from the sink in the corner of the room.

'You've done such a wonderful job,' Bryn says, and Sue, beside him, nods. 'It really is a beautiful thing you've given us.'

He has seen Bryn and Sue change from being kids to being adults *with* kids. He's been at their wedding, he's been at their parties, he's seen them spend a whole night in Cyprus, laughing until Sue wet herself. Richard has seen all this, but to have them here – together – in front of him, it's almost unreal. He wonders if this is what it'll be like to see Tommy Cooper later?

He brings them tea and they sit there in the small room, all three very close, and Richard thinks: how on earth did I ever get here?

'We've watched it four times this week,' Bryn says. 'I dun know how we'll ever repay you.'

Sue is smiling, too, but Richard can tell she doesn't want to be here, that being here only reminds her of what isn't in the film.

'Ah, I was just doing my job,' Richard says. 'It's just what we do.'

Bryn smiles a huge grin. 'Ah, it's more than that, though. It really is.'

There's a silent pause among them, and Richard feels strangely guilty that he's been paid for work that actually means something to someone else.

'Now, listen,' Bryn says, 'you're probably gonna think we're mad . . . But I've arranged for a little screening of our film, and I'd love it – absolutely love it – if you'd come. I mean, you made the thing – you should be there!'

As he sees them out to the car park, and Sue smiles weakly and waves goodbye, Richard thinks he should have felt worse for the times he cheated on Karen. And the thought grasps him; his insides narrow and flatten. He goes back into the office and plays his own Memory Tapes. He watches as a boy and a girl kiss on a bench outside Cardiff Odeon in 1990: his and Karen's first date.

*

He has no idea how Karen got the bandage on her arm. She and the kids are eating dinner and she hasn't mentioned it once. He hasn't been for a few days, so there's a chance that her arm mightn't even come up in conversation. But that's awful, isn't it? That he could miss an incident like that. Something terrible could happen, and he wouldn't even know.

He stays and he watches as Rhian sits on her bed, writing in her diary. He stays and he watches as Aled sprawls on his belly on the carpet, watching cartoons on the TV. He stays and he watches as Karen sits at the kitchen table, talking on the phone.

Then he remembers about tonight: Tommy Cooper.

By the time he arrives at the Workmen's Hall, the doors are closed and the man won't let him in. Besides, Lisa has the ticket and she's not answering her phone. He pictures it vibrating in her pocket – and her sitting in the audience, taking it out, looking at his glowing name, then putting it back into her bag.

The man tells him to wait until the interval.

Richard stands outside, leaning against the wall, and he thinks again about Karen's arm. His thoughts bundle up beside each other, and he wonders if Karen did it to herself.

When Lisa arrives back, he's on the couch, watching TV.

'I'm so sorry,' he says. 'I got stuck in work. Did you get my calls?'

'It's fine,' she says, and it's clear that it's not. 'You're the one who missed out.'

*

He senses the growing-apart. She spends more time on her phone, and he spends more time at work.

He becomes convinced she's cheating on him. But it doesn't make him angry or jealous, it just makes him sad.

*

On Rhian's birthday, he calls his boss and says he's sick. He files through security, gets in the lift, and goes to the first empty booth. He watches as Rhian's teacher cuts the cake and asks a boy to hand around small slices on blue napkins. He watches as Rhian's classmates gather round her in a circle. He watches as they all reach in and tug her hair nine times, and once more for luck. But the screen pauses, and the advert for the Full Package appears. It covers the screen, and the Scottish woman's voiceover – the one he's heard so many times – tells him that *registering couldn't be easier*.

When the footage returns, Rhian is in the corridor, her eyes red and burning, and her teacher tells her she's a brave girl, that everything will be okay.

He takes the next day off, too, and goes to the Booths first thing. He watches as Karen stands in the stairwell at her office and calls the insurance company. She often loses her temper on the phone, and he wishes he could be there now, to make the call on her behalf.

He watches for three hours straight. He doesn't even realise the time, until the bell sounds and the kids are leaving their classrooms and heading for the gate – where his father is waiting for them. He wants to watch them with his parents now. Karen can't seem to talk about him with the kids, so it's only when they're with his parents that they talk openly. When his daughter sees the school counsellor, she doesn't really say much, but with his mother, she's another person. She's expressive and speaks fluently about him, about her dreams and her nightmares – and his mother listens. And yes, last week his mother had to pretend to fetch something from upstairs because it was all too much – and he cried so hard and for so long that he was dehydrated and wholly spent – but Richard left the booth feeling lighter. As if this was something that he could learn to live with.

It's 4.30 now, and the kids are at his parents' kitchen table, eating yoghurts and telling stories about their day in school.

He selects his wife's channel – just for a moment, just to check in – and the screen expands, and there she is again, in the office car park now, the phone in her hand, a cigarette held to her lips.

'I understand that,' she says to the person on the phone. 'But that's *not* what you told me last week.'

He's never liked this tone of hers. He can't tell who she's speaking to, but he reckons she's made some mistake with the insurance form or a gas bill, and she's trying to cover for it. And he feels embarrassed for her, and embarrassed by her, too. If he were there now, they'd be arguing about it. Or they'd argue after she got off the phone. And he feels the missing of that – of the chance to fall out with her. And it's all so frustrating that he feels skittish, as if he has to get up and run or punch something.

When he gets home, there's a note from Lisa on the table:

Phone died. I've gone out with work people. See you in the morning. x

He turns on the TV, and watches a sitcom called *Three's a Cloud* – about a woman and her two husbands – but the show always ends up annoying him, and he turns it off before it's finished. He showers, goes to bed, and quickly falls asleep.

*

In the dream, a presence shows him everything. He's shown that beneath this world is the first world, his first life. There is a series of metal grids, like honeycombs, stacked crosswise, and if you get on your knees, you can peek through the holes and see the whole world below.

'There's something you should know,' the presence says. 'Your family are dead. What you're being shown at the Booths are only recordings. They've been dead a hundred years.'

In the dream, Richard can't work out if it makes a difference that they're dead. He tells the presence that he doesn't know whether it's true or not, but all the same, he'll still go and watch.

*

He wakes to music coming from the street – it sounds like 'Walking in the Air'. He gets up and draws back the curtain. Lisa's apartment overlooks the castle, and it takes a moment for the scene to etch itself as real: there are people out there on the moat. It has frozen over, and people in hats and scarves and coats are skating across the ice. He can hear the music clearly now. And across the moat, someone's right foot suddenly dips up into the air and they crash down onto the ice. Another person bends to pick up their friend, and though, from here, he can't see their features, he can tell that the two of them are laughing. And on the others go, skating in circuits.

He's never been ice-skating. Rhian had asked to go last Christmas to the Winter Wonderland in Cardiff, but he'd always been afraid of it, afraid of falling and breaking a leg or an arm. So Karen took her to the outdoor rink, and he and Aled went to the cinema. Was that his problem, he wonders, that he didn't push himself enough? At the start, Karen joked that he always took the easy way out of things, but as the years passed, the joke hardened into something else: an unstated accusation. And where she once saw and understood his fears, he felt that she began to see them as stubbornness and something else instead. He looks at the skaters again, and he tries to picture himself out there on the ice. The scene resembles a painting he once saw, but he doesn't remember where.

When he goes to the kitchen, Lisa is sitting on her chair with her feet up, looking at her phone.

'What you watching?' he says.

'Oh, just the usual crap,' she says and she folds the phone and puts it down on the table.

'D'you fancy going ice-skating?' he says. 'You won't believe it, but I've never actually been.'

'I'd love to,' she says, 'but they need me in work this afternoon.'

'Really?'

'Yeah,' she says. 'I'm pissed off to be honest. But it's money, isn't it?' Her phone beeps and vibrates on the table. Richard stares at it. 'Yeah,' she says. 'And we could do with some extra money, couldn't we?'

'You gonna look at your phone?' he says.

'It's probably only work.'

Right, he thinks, and the whole thing unfurls. He pictures it all, this other man she's seeing. He is taller than him, and his body is firm, and he is assertive and he has a long, strong dick, and he is everything that Richard isn't.

When she leaves the house, Richard goes to Tesco and buys a shoulder of vodka.

Through the teeming rain he goes, and it feels like he has drilled to the core and all that's left is oil, and it's gushing inside, and if it doesn't come out, he'll combust. At the Care Centre, he finds himself pacing back and forth. His blood feels hot in his veins, and he can't tell if his arms are damp from sweat or the soaked-in rain. Through the window, he can see and hear children running about, little kids on little bikes, and older ones sitting at tables, doing jigsaws, eating crisps, playing computer games. And he sees Sue and Bryn, too. They're sat on the edge of their chairs, watching the kids play. Beside them he sees the back of a woman, Lisa's frame and size, bouncing a toddler on her lap. Richard imagines composing himself, going inside, removing his shoes, laying his socks on a radiator, and walking barefoot across the wooden floor.

A boy – eighteen or so – sees Richard at the window. He makes a gesture and Richard shakes his head. But still the boy comes to the door.

'Why don't you come in?' he says. 'It's lovely and dry.'

'I'm alright,' Richard says. The boy has a kind and solid face, he thinks. He's wearing a green polo shirt, and Richard can picture him working in a garden centre, pushing bulbs into soil.

'Don't be stupid, mun,' the boy says. 'Come and have a cuppa tea.'

'I can't,' Richard says. He can feel the boy taking his features in, working out his story.

'How old are yours?' the boy says.

'I've got to go now,' Richard says

But the woman at the Viewing Booths won't let him in.

'You know the rules,' she says, and she rubs her leather gloves together. 'We can't be having people drunk in there. It's tough enough as it is.'

'Come on,' Richard says. 'I'm alright. I'm in a good place, I really am.'

'No good arguing,' she says. 'Get yourself a coffee, then try again in an hour.'

'Look,' Richard says. 'I need to see my kids.'

'No can do,' the guard says. 'I told you, come back in an hour.'

'It's my daughter's birthday,' he says. 'I just want to see her on her birthday. It's her first without me.'

'How old is she?'

'She's nine today.'

The woman looks the other way, then thumbs Richard in. 'I haven't seen you, alright?'

Richard finds a booth, settles down, and watches. He watches as his wife and kids sit on the living-room floor, playing Hungry Hippos. His bladder is full and he can feel it pressing, but he keeps watching, keeps watching until Aled has won and they are all cheering and Aled has his hands pumping in the air.

He's on his way to the bathroom when he hears shuffling and moaning from another booth. The person sounds in agony. He'd usually leave them, but he is drunk, and when he's drunk he wants to save the world. He goes to their booth and calls out.

The door opens, and there's a woman sat there, her jeans and knickers around her ankles. She is masturbating, tears filling her eyes.

'He just told her he loved her,' the woman says. Onscreen, a man is taking another woman from behind.

Richard helps her put her clothes back on, and guides her to the cafe on Level 1. He buys her a coffee and a piece of carrot cake. She is shaking and she doesn't eat a bite.

'How long have you been here?' he says.

But she says nothing, just sits there, her eyes cast down. Richard moves his hand to hers. She looks up at him, and very quietly she says: 'Will you have sex with me, please?'

'You don't want that,' he says, shaking his head. 'You just need to go home. Where do you live? I'll walk you.'

Her place is almost identical to Lisa's: the same pine floors, the crisp white walls, the tall windows facing out onto town. But the flat is filled with photos taken at the Booths: her boyfriend in a Liverpool shirt, her boyfriend lying topless in bed, her boyfriend in a suit at a friend's wedding.

Richard makes coffee, but she adds whiskey to both mugs. She tells him how she used be a Christian, but now, well, what's the point?

They kiss, but stop when she begins to cry. They lie on the couch, her head on his shoulder. When she falls asleep, he lies there for five, ten, fifteen minutes, then leaves.

*

'How did Dad actually die?' Rhian asks one day, and Karen tells her that he just fell asleep and never woke up. It's a stupid thing to tell a kid, but Richard knows Karen was only panicking.

But now Rhian is scared to go to bed. She spends the nights awake, and the days in a gust of fatigue. And now Aled is lying in bed crying. He says the bed covers are pulled too tightly around him. He says he thinks he's going to die.

*

In work, Richard starts watching his Memory Tapes. At first, he only watches when he arrives in the morning. And then he begins to watch the tapes in his lunch hour, too. It's like a reward. Each time he completes a scene of someone else's film, he watches a scene from his own. Sometimes, when his boss is away, he'll put a chair in front of the door, and masturbate to Memory Tapes of him and Karen. Other times, he'll think of a random memory, then load the file.

There he is: fifteen, on a bus, coming back from a geography trip in North Wales, holding hands with Helen Evans. There he is: his twentieth birthday, outside Chippy Alley in Cardiff, puking all the over place. There he is: in the hospital, Rhian being born; Karen is exhausted and not talking to him, and Rhian's little hand is holding his pinky finger. And it all comes back now: it flows, it gushes, and it fills him with love and all he can think is I'm sorry I'm sorry I'm so fucking sorry.

*

He's behind with work. The sick days have set him back, and he just can't focus any more. It all feels like such a fucking waste.

Yes, he shouldn't be here. He's got his own children, his own family. He should be at home with his kids now. He should be helping Aled with a jigsaw. He should be reading Rhian a story, or helping her wash her hair, or taking them all out on a trip to the park, or the beach, though they never really did go to the beach. The beach was always so far away.

He never gave them enough time. If he's honest, he

didn't know how to love them. How to love Karen. When he was with them, he got it, he understood. But when he was away, when he was away with work, he didn't miss them. Not really. He was glad of the space. But they never felt real to him. They just felt like something that had happened to a version of him, some other him, some unreal part of him that he couldn't fully receive or understand. It's why the affairs started, he thinks, why he never felt the guilt. But they had always been there, these feelings of distance. It was the same growing up. When he moved away, he didn't miss his parents. And whenever he told someone he loved them, it wasn't true, not really. It was just something he said to match their expectations. And now Lisa, what is all that about? Does she even like him? And how does he *actually* feel about her? He doesn't know, not really.

There are parts of him he doesn't understand, parts he wilfully hides from himself.

*

He has the dream again, the dream that the footage at the Booths is recorded, that his family are already dead, that a hundred years have passed. In the dream, he's in the editing suite – but the editing suite is in his primary school – and the presence tells him that there is a way out, that it's hidden in the basement. He runs to the schoolyard, and jumps the gate that leads to the basement. He runs down the concrete stairs, and his legs feel empty. There's a bare ceiling, a tangle of cables and wires hanging over the corridor. He pushes through and he can see the door up ahead, a line of light under it. There are workmen in the corner, and they're sitting and they're smoking. They are watching him, but they don't seem to care.

He can hear music, carol singers outside. He pushes through the corridor. He keeps pushing and running, and no one tries to stop him. He reaches the door and he feels it opening; there's blue sky and there's nothing, except a falling, like how it feels when you miss the last step on the stairs. And that feeling stretches – and he is lifting and he is floating – and he is above Caerphilly, above the town, watching the shops and the houses and the castle shrink, and he is high above the mountains now, and he is lifting and he is almost home.

*

He doesn't remember how the idea came, but come it did. He took her details this morning, and here he is, loading Lisa's Memory Tapes. He goes to the last scene and rewinds: Lisa at a kids' party. It's summer, and it's a big house, and she's in the garden and she's dressed like a clown. She's making balloon animals for the kids, and they are laughing and screaming and asking her to make all sorts of animals, and she is laughing, too. She is making jokes, and the kids are eating ice cream, and she is taking cash from the birthday girl's mother, and now she is talking to someone, it seems like her boss, no, it's her sister, her sister is her boss, her sister runs the party company, and they're arguing now, they're arguing about petrol money, or expenses, or something like that – he can't quite work out what – and she's getting in the car, and she is angry, and she is driving, and bang – lorry.

He goes back.

He rewinds to before the party.

And there Lisa is, she's in a house, it seems like her house, and she is carrying a kid, a girl, about two or two and a half, and she is carrying her, and an older man comes to the door, and it's her father, and he's coming in, and he's coming to look after the girl. And the little girl is asleep, and Lisa is leaving now; she kisses the child on the head and she says, 'Goodbye baby girl, Mummy loves you and she'll be back in a bit.'

*

Bryn is beaming and thanking everyone for coming. They're in the dining hall of the castle, where chairs have been set up for everyone. The film is projected onto a white screen on the far wall, and everyone sits transfixed in a way that surprises Richard. He always thought that people wouldn't want to watch other people's films – that it'd be like looking at someone else's holiday photos or listening to their dreams: only tolerated so that others will watch and listen to ours in turn. But no, at the end of the film, as Sue's coffin is slowly being ushered behind the crematorium curtain, there's a hush, a reverence, like everyone in the castle is at the funeral itself. Richard looks around, and all eyes are fixed at the film.

'Well,' Sue shouts, 'if I'd known it took so long for the coffin to burn, I'd have got myself buried.'

But nobody laughs. On the screen, her coffin disappears, and a school choir sings 'Ar Lan y Môr', and all the people in the castle begin to sing it, too. And the shivers run through Richard now. He's flushed with it, that deep, deep shame.

When the film ends, Bryn rises and he gets Sue to stand, too. He takes off his glasses and wipes his eyes.

'I still can't believe it,' he says. 'I can't believe you're actually here.' He puts his arm around his wife and pulls her close.

*

That night, when Richard tells Lisa that he knows about her daughter, that he saw it on the tapes, she begins to breath very rapidly and starts slapping herself across the face. 'No,' she says, 'no, no, no.' She bolts to the bathroom and locks herself in. He stands at the door and tries talking to her, but she turns on the taps, and his voice is drowned by the sound of running water. When she eventually comes out, she says, as if she's chosen each word very carefully:

'I want you to listen. Just once in your life, listen. You don't know everything and you're not always right. You are cold and you are distant and you've never given, and I have never fully—'

'But the girl—'

'I'm not going to talk to you about my daughter,' she says. 'I am going back to the bathroom and when I come out I want you gone.'

So he moves back into the tiny apartment beside the train station, where each night the windows rattle as another batch of people comes into the town. He lives there alone, visiting the Viewing Booths whenever he's not at work. The months pass and the seasons change, and he is finally able to afford the Full Package. He buys the app for his phone, and each night when he gets into bed, he lies there, his back propped with a pillow, and watches his first life flickering on the screen, like the last embers of a star that's died but whose light softly whispers: *nos da, nos da, nos da.*

*

And months later again, he runs into Lisa at the Viewing Booths. She tells him that she has left the cafe and she's working at the Care Centre now.

'All those kids there,' she says. 'It'd break your heart. The toddlers are the worst. They cry out for their mummy all the time. But it's better than selling sandwiches.'

'I am sorry, you know,' he says. 'I shouldn't have—'

'No,' she says, 'but you did.'

They go to the cafe on Level 1 and they talk and they talk. They stay up late and they unload to one another, tell each other things they never said when they were together. And Richard wonders why this happens, why he can't just be honest with the person he's in a relationship with; why he spends so much time not even being honest with himself. They make plans to meet again, and in the morning he receives a text:

So, shall we?

It's a cold day as he moves through crowds of people in coats and scarves. He meets Lisa at the picnic table, and she is smiling in a knowing way, though he can't be sure what it is she knows. The wind whips at his cheeks, and he can feel the blood rising as they walk along the path. The smell of meat drifts from the hotdog stand, and they walk side by side, neither saying much at all.

At the skate stall, they pay their money, remove their shoes and put on the blades. He looks to the moat. People are dashing by, circling and stopping and changing direction, and they make it look so easy, but still, it looks impossible. She takes his hand and they walk towards the rink. Caerphilly Castle looms above, and the sky is white and full of something, or maybe nothing, but to him it does seem endless.

He is clinging to the rail now and he just wants to collapse. He just wants to fall to his knees and stay there, on the firm ground. He doesn't know if he can go through with it. *Leave me*, he wants to say. *Just go and leave me here*. But she takes his hand again, and together they walk to the entrance and Richard steps onto the ice.

'Slow,' she whispers. 'We'll take it slow.'

DIOLCH YN FAWR

These stories have had many early friends and readers. So, thanks to: Lisa, Sally, Lauren, Rachel, Gill, Tim, Sam, Berwyn, Toby, Nicole, Dave O'Carroll, Liam, Felim, Conor, Judith, Tramp Press, Sara, Antony & Sean Farrell, Viv, Ann Kenny, Colm Farren, Michael Ray, Declan, Colin, Mary, Aled, Jenna, Lorella, Lorenzo, John Kenny, Kevin Breathnach, John Lavin, Aida Birch, Will and Hilary. Thanks also to Andrew, Jean, James, Henry, Tommy and my classmates at UEA.

'The Lover' by Joy Williams provided the spark for 'Castle View'.

I am indebted (hopefully not literally) to Arts Council Ireland for their generous financial support in 2012 and 2014.

I'm thankful and wholly grateful to John Boyne & Ali Smith for the early encouragement and support. I feel extraordinarily fortunate to be looked after by Tracy Bohan and Hannah Griffiths – for their belief, sound guidance and for making publication so painless. Ditto Catrin Evans & Alex Russell. A debt of gratitude is also owed to Will Atkins, Luke Bird, Kate McQuaid, Kate Ward, Katie Hall and everyone at Faber.

With thanks to the boys.

With so much thanks to my family.